THE FINAL UNFINISHED VOYAGE
OF JACK AUBREY

Patrick O'Brian is the author of the acclaimed Aubrey–Maturin tales and the biographer of Joseph Banks and Picasso. His first novel, *Testimonies,* and his *Collected Short Stories* have recently been reprinted by HarperCollins. He translated many works from French into English, among them the novels and memoirs of Simone de Beauvoir and the first volume of Jean Lacouture's biography of Charles de Gaulle. In 1995 he was the first recipient of the Heywood Hill Prize for a lifetime's contribution to literature. In the same year he was also awarded the CBE. In 1997 he was awarded an honorary doctorate of letters by Trinity College, Dublin. He died in January 2000 at the age of 85.

The Works of Patrick O'Brian

The Aubrey/Maturin Novels
In order of publication

Novels

Tales

Biography

Anthology

PATRICK O'BRIAN

The Final Unfinished Voyage of Jack Aubrey

HarperCollins*Publishers*

HarperCollins*Publishers*
1 London Bridge Street,
London SE1 9GF

www.harpercollins.co.uk

This paperback edition 2010
10

First published in Great Britain by HarperCollins*Publishers* 2004

A catalogue record for this book is available from the British Library

ISBN 978 0 00 735843 4

Set in New Baskerville

Printed and bound by CPI Group (UK) Ltd, Croydon CR0 4YY

Contents

Editor's Note

When Patrick O'Brian died in early January 2000, he left 65 handwritten pages of the untitled twenty-first novel in the Aubrey/Maturin series. He had also begun typing the same material and had made revisions to the typescript.

The printed version here presented follows the author's revised typescript, with the correction of a few obvious omissions and errors of spelling. But it is not to be supposed that these pages are exactly as O'Brian would have wanted them to be in a final draft, or had he seen proofs of his book. There are occasional word repetitions and rhyming echoes that he would surely have caught on subsequent readings. The typescript ends in mid-sentence (page 74), and chapter 3 continues – without conclusion – in O'Brian's own hand. The facsimile pages include such wonderful curiosities as O'Brian's sketch of the seating arrangements for a dinner party, and the reader is granted a last, intimate glimpse of this extraordinary writer practising his craft.

Foreword by William Waldegrave

This book contains a fragment. It is the beginning of a beginning of Patrick O'Brian's twenty-first novel, left uncompleted at his death. We do not know the shape of the story he had planned; he left no outline or sketch. We do not have a finished version of any of the three chapters, the manuscript and typescript of which are reproduced here. Much further perfectionist, painstaking work would have gone on before that eagle eye would have been satisfied.

But what we do have is of extraordinary interest to lovers of O'Brian's magnificent naval series. The personal glimpse we get of this intensely private man at work is both moving and impressive. We see a master craftsman, still in full possession of his craft, pressing on, even in old age, with the same dedication and courage which, through a long life containing many set-backs and vicissitudes, brought him in the end to fame and success.

It is rather as if we had opened the door to the studio of a great painter and found that he had left a canvas on the easel, almost entirely untouched – this is not one of those painters who sketch in the whole and then overpaint – but with one corner glowing with some fine colours. Some detail is already there, worked up; some brush strokes are clearly sketched, to be revisited; others point to the architecture of the whole and give an inkling of what the completed structure might have looked like.

Most touchingly, as in the margins of Edward Lear watercolours, we also find personal little notes and memoranda written to himself; there he is, suddenly, Patrick O'Brian himself, rubbing shoulders on the page with Jack Aubrey and Stephen Maturin in the same fine handwriting.

Uncovering the way in which O'Brian writes is a task for the professional literary scholar, not for me. But, looking at these manuscript pages, and at the typescript, certain conclusions seem to suggest themselves.

First, O'Brian seems to work at several levels in terms of completeness at the same time. On one level, the frontier of the story is pushed forward boldly, with a broad brush – surely leaving behind gaps for later infilling. Thus we sweep across the southern Atlantic from the Strait of Magellan to the coast of South Africa, providing a structure for the first quarter or so of the book in outline, but leaving plenty of room for the insertion not only of detail but also, and without difficulty, of quite substantial further episodes.

Then, at another level of finish, there are episodes well worked up and broadly complete, like the meeting between Jack and his black papal nuncio son, Sam, in Buenos Aires. Here, more polishing undoubtedly would have been done, but I would be surprised if anything much would have changed.

Finally, there are paragraphs not only worked up but perfect and complete. Take the moment – so central to Jack's life-long ambition – when his rear-admiral's flag is finally broken out at the mizzen of his own first flagship:

> 'The folded bundle soared aloft, followed with the utmost concentration by all hands: at exactly the right moment, the exact height to an inch, the coxswain snapped the tie and the rear-admiral's blue flag streamed out bravely in the wind, instantly greeted by the first of thirteen solemn guns, enormously loud, salutes from all the members of the squadron, distant cheering from *Surprise* and clouds of wheeling, discontented gulls.'

This seems to me perfect, but it has taken many careful revisions to achieve, with the seagulls, in particular, overpainted again and again: 'uneasy', 'complaining', 'querulous' are all tried for size, but to my ear the typescript version is best and would surely have remained.

So that square inch or two of the canvas is finished, almost unvarnished, while the majority remains quite blank, and surrounding areas are only sketched and touched in.

If I am right, and O'Brian is pushing forward the story at different levels of completeness at the same time, with almost everything subject to revision, and with the possibility of considerable revisions (these unfinished chapters are, after all, a good deal shorter than most of those in the completed books), it is worth pausing for a moment on the themes which these early chapters promise. We can allow ourselves the luxury of dreaming about what might have been the elements of this story.

Some are well signalled. Lord Leyton is obviously going to be a choleric and difficult commander-in-chief. If Jack could lose his temper so dangerously all those years before in the Admiralty boardroom with Lord St Vincent himself, how much more danger is there of ructions and rows with Lord Leyton?

Then there is Maturin's flowering relationship with the intelligent, long-legged naturalist, Christine: is Maturin at last to find unclouded happiness? The hope inclines one to make the sign against the evil eye, sharing the superstition of the sailors; so often O'Brian, who in so many ways models Maturin closely upon himself, seems to inflict disaster on his fictional alter ego.

And we are on the way to the Cape, taken not so long ago from the Dutch, and then, as now, a hotbed of complex politics and, of course, a paradise for the botanist and naturalist. I am sure Stephen would have encountered an oryx, at least. The fleet is to be based at the Cape to protect the India and China trade: pirates, opium and perhaps Burmese adventures lie without too much anachronism to the east.

But to the west lies one place about which surely we are meant to hear more, whether on the way to the Cape or later: St Helena. Can we really have Jack and Stephen within range of the imprisoned Napoleon without some encounter? Indeed, Lord Leyton announces that he will interview the unfortunate Emperor and explain to him how he might have won the battle of Waterloo.

What is more, O'Brian, like Marryat and Forester before him, borrows freely from the extraordinary career of Thomas Cochrane, Lord Dundonald, the greatest frigate captain of the age. Cochrane went to Chile and Brazil for the same purpose as did Aubrey in *Blue at the Mizzen*, and their adventures are not dissimilar. Cochrane never actually called on Napoleon (who called him 'that sea wolf') but he planned to do so, and in the most extraordinary circumstances. He concocted a harebrained scheme for rescuing the great man and carrying him off to Brazil, there to install him as the Emperor of South America, a scheme which, not surprisingly, was never brought to fruition (though history would have been much more fun if it had been).

While Cochrane was a radical, who still admired Napoleon for his revolutionary youth, Jack Aubrey is a Tory through and through, and Maturin hates Napoleon, whose secret police have tortured him, and considers him a tyrant who has destroyed the small nations of Europe. No scheme of Cochrane's type would have been entertained for a moment on board HMS *Suffolk*. But I still cannot imagine that we should have not had some encounter. We will never know.

The fascination of these pages lies in the privilege they give us of seeing, most intimately, the master at work. There is sadness in it: his beloved wife Mary had died, and she was the background to the whole of his mature writing life. She typed his manuscripts and, I suspect, discussed them with him. Without Mary, he could not manage the house in French Catalan Collioure; so he was no longer working in the familiar cave-like writing-room under the house that he had himself largely designed and built, with everything to hand exactly where he wanted it.

We see him now struggling to keep at least two manuscript versions in order, clearly doing his own typing, somewhat erratically, and sometimes apparently composing directly onto the typewriter as well as with the pen. Some manuscript pages are fair copies, in a strong clear hand, others are not. There are overlapping pages, repetitions, excisions, notes to himself. There is a considerable episode (the duel which Maturin fights) which is not yet in the typescript at all. There are distressing notes at the end where he thinks he has lost some of chapter three (and suspects – in a phrase that is pure Maturin – 'a malignant hand'). Evidently, it was found again, because here we have it with the table plan for Lord Leyton's dinner in the margin, just as he describes.

It is impossible not to be moved by the courage and anxiety of O'Brian, now an old man and alone (though, to his infinite pleasure, pride and gratitude, sheltered and honoured by Trinity College, Dublin), as he tries to keep his pages in order, writes notes about the need for more ink-cartridges for his pen, and on one page writes, very small, 'I am absurdly sleepy', in the way that medieval scribes sometimes wrote comments about the weather or their health in the margins of the illuminated manuscripts on which they were working.

It is the courage that is most striking: the discipline, the will. He has no intention of retiring or throwing in the towel. I leave it to the reader to judge, but out of these fragments, these very fragmentary fragments, I have no doubt that another fine story would have been built if he had had time.

Part of the strength, it might seem, flows back from the very characters he has himself created. It is as if these old friends offer their author comfort. Not for him the prickly and hostile relationship between Conan Doyle and Sherlock Holmes. O'Brian does not want to push Aubrey or Maturin over the Reichenbach falls in order to free himself of their tyranny, as Conan Doyle (unsuccessfully) did Holmes, in order to return the spotlight to such books as *The White Company* which he thought his best.

On the contrary, O'Brian loves Aubrey, and is increasingly indistinguishable from Maturin who loves Aubrey too. It is impossible for those of us who were lucky enough to know him not to hear O'Brian in every sentence of Maturin – and vice versa. Such speculation is dangerous, but perhaps we can catch a faint echo, in the opening passage of chapter one, where Maturin struggles with paper and pens and fusses about completing a letter to Christine, of O'Brian's own efforts to restore order to his recalcitrant ring-binders. But we should be careful: O'Brian, like all great artists, had a powerful and concentrated will, and there was no more self-pity in him than there is in Maturin.

Nevertheless, in these pages it is perhaps not too fanciful to imagine that O'Brian has accorded himself the comfort of slipping into the world he has created in order to take refuge among his characters: gossiping with them about old adventures and planning out with them new stories. Sitting with them, perhaps, in the new rear-admiral's great cabin over a bottle or two of that lovely claret he delighted to pretend was 'un petit vin de famille' – Chateau Haut Brion.

I have said that it seems to my unprofessional eye that what we read here is not a first or second draft of something which would necessarily remain in this shape, awaiting only polishing. Rather, if I am right, we have some finished paragraphs set in a sketched structure which itself might well have been revisited (to accommodate Napoleon, for example), expanded, contracted, pushed about until he had his twelve or fourteen chapters roughed in, and then all to be redone again to the level of perfectionism which would have satisfied him. To return to my analogy of the painter, reading these pages is like watching the master getting out his brushes, mixing his colours, preparing his canvas, starting to paint one part of his great design, sketching a little, revisiting and working up some corner which has already gone well.

It is not like uncovering one perfect incomplete section cut from a finished canvas; we should not judge it like that; but characteristic brush strokes of the master are there. I delight in the unexpected adjectives, which hint at other little stories or digressions which could be followed up if you so wished: 'improbably quantities of port'; a 'shameless wombat'. I love the unexplained mystery of the obscurely strewn drowned dogs, not to mention the cabbage-selling werewolf on page 17. Sometimes you can see a tiny change made that transforms the first sketch into the finished O'Brian: how much better surely is 'seventy of the finest guinea pigs' than the first draft's 'some. . .' And how typical of O'Brian to enjoy the somewhat shocking fact (to English sensibilities at least) that in parts of Latin America our children's furry friends are indeed a delicacy on which one dines.

Imagine ourselves as literary scholars of the thirty-first century, experts in textural reconstruction. All O'Brian's completed books have been lost like the scrolls of Sappho's lyric poetry in some future equivalent of the Christian burning of the library of Alexandria or the Crusader sacking of Byzantium. By chance, only this book has survived. We future scholars would be intrigued, and a little puzzled. How could so many first-rank critics and so many excellent fellow novelists (their reviews have somehow survived my putative literary holocaust) have acclaimed O'Brian as the greatest historical novelist of his age? Or, as some would have it, of any age?

At first, we would find it hard to understand. But then the best of us, some future TJ Binyon or John Bailey, would get it. They would draw attention to the completed and polished paragraphs, where we have them, and ask us to imagine a whole book written in such elegant, exact and evocative prose – rather as we take the few lines we have left of Sappho and imagine the lost volumes of her poetry.

They would see at once the depth of learning – about history, the Royal Navy of the time, the scientific knowledge of the time (particularly natural history, medicine and astronomy) – worn so lightly but deployed so securely. (See how he grounds his description of the birds of the Strait of Magellan on Darwin himself in the note to page 7 of the manuscript. [*MS I, 6*])

They would grasp at once the sense of historical drama, the sweep of great events in the background, setting off the passionate commitment to the individuality of the *dramatis personae* in the foreground.

They would understand the sympathy for the close-knit community of a sailing warship – that mixture of camaraderie and claustrophobia caught so brilliantly by Peter Weir's film *Master and Commander: the Far Side of the World.*

They would see the humour just under the surface of so much of the writing: the sort of joke implied by the 'almost' in the Argentine official's suspicions that these northerners are 'given to cursing the Holy Father almost every day'. They would suspect that O'Brian was a writer who could make us laugh as well as cry.

They would not be able to imagine the full riches from this fragment, of course, any more than we can imagine everything that lay behind Sappho's reputation in antiquity from the bits and pieces which have survived. Nor would they be able to imagine the sheer tension of the sea chases in the completed books – page after page as that relentless Dutchman pursues them through the mountainous seas of the roaring forties in *Desolation Island.*

Perhaps, brought up short, for example, by that werewolf, they might have wondered about O'Brian's interest in taking us down strange, almost ghostly, unexpected pathways of the imagination – and noted the contrast between those surreal and beautiful episodes and the robust realism of his picture of life in the pubs and clubs of a smelly and raucous Regency England. But surely, no one would guess quite the otherworldly and lyrical beauty of the picture he conjures of a Buddhist Garden of Eden, in which live the charming orang-utans of *The Thirteen-Gun Salute* – a picture, O'Brian once told me, which was based on nothing other than his pure and extraordinary imagination.

They would not be able to predict the brilliance of the sustained comic writing of passages like the fox-hunt in *Master and Commander*, where both Aubrey and Maturin first meet Diana (the oxen nearly cutting a caper of their own at the end of that episode are my favourite oxen in literature).

Nothing yet written in the first workings for the twenty-first book would have shown them O'Brian's heart-wrenching capacity to depict friendship under the extreme pressures of battle, storm, triumph, disaster and the rivalries of love which makes the Aubrey–Maturin relationship one of the great creations of literature.

However, I would be willing to bet that plenty of these things and many others which we, the readers who do have access to those other twenty finished books, know so well, would also have been there in number twenty-one if it had been finished.

So it is fitting, as we close this last book, to give thanks for what Patrick O'Brian did complete and to celebrate a magnificent life's work. From the extraordinary juvenile books, through *Testimonies* and the short stories, to the translations, the wonderful Picasso biography, *Joseph Banks*, the two Anson novels (the first of which is as good as anything he wrote) and then to the crowning achievement of the twenty completed Aubrey–Maturin novels, it is a body of work to stand comparison with any.

In the margin of page 49 [*MS III, 16*] of the manuscript, he notes down words which show he is thinking about Macbeth's famous speech on death and reputation:

> *Tomorrow, and tomorrow and tomorrow,*
> *Creeps in this petty pace from day to day,*
> *To the last syllable of recorded time;*
> *And all our yesterdays have lighted fools*
> *The way to dusty death. . .*

But, on the evidence of this last fragment of O'Brian, he was not surrendering, not giving up the ghost. He had another book to write, or perhaps two. He had his craft, his skill, his scholarship, his imagination, his humour, his strong sense of honour – and his courage. When he thinks he has lost much of what he has written, he writes to himself on the last page that he may be able to rebuild the missing pages, but 'I shall have tea first and concentrate what wits I still possess.'

Complex and subtle he was: but he was no despairing Macbeth. Rather he was like the aged Ulysses, Aubrey's ultimate literary forebear, in Tennyson's poem, setting off once again with undaunted spirit into the unknown:

Old age hath yet his honour and his toil;
Death closes all: but something ere the end
Some work of noble note may yet be done,
Not unbecoming men that strove with Gods. . .

I hope that last tea was a good one – like the one the three little girls sought on page 63 [*MS III, 9*], 'with cake or at least muffin'.

Never did a writer deserve it more, nor the gratitude and affection of his readers throughout the world.

THE FINAL
UNFINISHED VOYAGE
OF JACK AUBREY

The sails of a square-rigged ship, hung out to dry in a calm.

1   Flying jib
2   Jib
3   Fore topmast staysail
4   Fore staysail
5   Foresail, or course
6   Fore topsail
7   Fore topgallant
8   Mainstaysail
9   Main topmast staysail
10 Middle staysail
11 Main topgallant staysail

12 Mainsail, or course
13 Maintopsail
14 Main topgallant
15 Mizzen staysail
16 Mizzen topmast staysail
17 Mizzen topgallant staysail
18 Mizzen sail
19 Spanker
20 Mizzen topsail
21 Mizzen topgallant

Illustration source: Serres, Liber Nauticus.
Courtesy of The Science and Technology Research Center,
The New York Public Library, Astor, Lenox, and Tilden Foundation

Chapter One

Stephen Maturin squared up to his writing-desk once more: he had been called away to attend to one of the ship's boys who in the lightness of his heart had contrived to stun himself in the foretop by taking the maul from its place, tossing it to a considerable height and so misjudging the revolutions as it fell that the massive head struck him down, speechless and unnaturally pale. Stephen dressed the wound, such as it was (more bruise than blood and no bone broken) and said to his loblolly-boy, 'Tell Dr Jacob, when he comes back, that this boy is to have no grog for the next three days, and tomorrow he may keep his hammock.' Dr Jacob, the surgeon's mate, was away visiting friends aboard the frigate's tender, the rapid and windwardly Chesapeake schooner *Ringle*, and Stephen glanced in her direction, fine on the starboard bow, before going down from the brilliance of noon to the comparatively sombre cabin that he shared with Captain Aubrey.

He had already written *My dear Christine* before he was called away, and he had dated the letter *Surprise,*

* The marginal note indicates where, in the text narrative, the beginning of each facsimile page of manuscript occurs.

at sea, in Magellan's Strait. At his first sitting down he had meant to tell her, with what skill he could command, of the extraordinary beauty of the weather and of the Strait, generally so forbidding: he should certainly have spoken of the favourable wind that had allowed them to keep topgallantsails abroad ever since the morning watch; but above all he should have dwelt upon the happiness that filled the ship, homeward bound after a very long, arduous and most uncommonly dangerous voyage, a well-found ship commanded by a right seaman, a well-liked, deeply-respected fighting captain who, moreover, was soon to hoist his flag. There was no secret about this: Jack Aubrey's first unrestrained cries of delight on receipt of the blessed order had not escaped his steward nor anyone else within a range of twenty yards: nor had the unwonted floods of rum, the feasts in cabin, gunroom and midshipmen's berth; and the sacred blue flag itself, the mark of a rear-admiral, lay openly on the fo'c'sle, shaded from too fierce a sun, from untimely drops of spray, by an awning, the sail-maker and his mates, the ship's tailor and his, titivating it with minute stitches, while every hand aboard added half an inch of seam around its ample verge. It was considered the handsomest ensign in the service.

MS I, 2

But for the moment the flag was absent from Stephen's mind: indeed the mind itself was in a singular state of absence, hesitation, even stupidity. Before being called to the wretched boy, he had known at least the general trend of the passages that were to follow the words that lay there before him; but now he was filled with doubt, and to give his wits time to settle and clarify he mended his pen, clipping its tip with a minute pair of metal jaws made for the purpose and trimming the sides with a lancet capable of splitting hairs.

Yet the right free, easy, candid expressions would not come, though the Christine in question was very dear to him: Stephen had long practised medicine, a calling in which discretion is often of great importance; but for an even longer time, if time is to be measured by stress, he had been an intelligence-agent, and here discretion was of the very essence, since an unguarded word or step might lead to the agent's death and to the death, the often hideous death, of his friends and the destruction of their cause.

He sat down, his expression still tolerably blank: he was a lean, middle-sized man, unremarkable, of mixed Catalan and Irish origin; but it was the tropical sun and the sea-air that accounted for his dark complexion, not any mixture of Moorish blood, for although his birth was illegitimate (which weighed upon him) his ancestors had been Christians time out of mind. A man of something less than forty, though he looked older as his mind wrestled with the difficulties of giving the intelligent woman he longed to marry a coherent, plausible account of the *Surprise*'s activities and of her present return, mission accomplished: for as soon as Captain Aubrey joined the South African squadron in the River Plate, going aboard HMS *Suffolk*, taking command of her and hoisting or causing to be hoisted the flag, blue at the mizzen, her act would turn him into that glorious creature a rear-admiral, the likelihood, the virtual

MS I, 3

5

certainty, was that *Surprise* should return to England, carrying Jack Aubrey's official dispatch, two young men who were to pass for lieutenant and a great number of papers and certificates from the bosun, carpenter, gunner and purser justifying the expenditure or replacement of almost every item in the ship's unbelievably complex gear, furnishings and supplies, from pistol-flints to great round-shot and innumerable blocks. There was also a flat, factual, unadorned account of the *Surprise*'s meetings with the Chilean authorities and of her proceedings, together with volume after volume of her activity in charting and surveying the South American islands and coasts.

She was one of the smaller frigates, carrying no more than 28 great guns, and although in the right hands she was an outstanding sailer she had been sold out of the service when heavier craft were built and Stephen had bought her: so there she was, eminently seaworthy and available for hire to the Hydrographical Service of the Admiralty once Napoleon had been dealt with and the western world was at something like peace.

Her ostensible function was to survey and chart the little-known coasts and innumerable islands of the recently independent republic of Chile and to help form its navy, training the young officers. All this was perfectly avowable and even praiseworthy, but the voyage had other aspects that were never distinctly laid down in written orders but that were implied and understood on either side: and here total candour was wholly out of the question, so that Stephen's letter home could obviously not be all he wished.

In the first place, through Stephen's innumerable connexions, Jack had been appointed commander-in-chief of the Chilean navy as well as Admiralty hydrographer; but the frigate's voyage had been slow (very foul weather south of the Horn) and when she reached Chile she found that the situation had changed remarkably. Apart from anything else she was met with a bewildering number of juntas, of more or less independent governing bodies belonging to widely differing political parties, one of which had appointed its own commander-in-chief though all were obsessed by the fear of a Peruvian invasion by land or sea or both: Peru was still ruled by the Spanish king's viceroy in Lima, and it still possessed a powerful, well-trained navy.

MS I, 3a
*MS I, 4**

After a very great number of vicissitudes, changes of ministry and so on it appeared to Jack that since his main duty, often expressed in London but never committed to writing, was to preserve the independent Chilean republic, the best way of doing so and at the same time of protecting his beloved infant Chilean navy was to attack the Peruvians in their port of Callao and if possible to cut out their powerful frigate *Esmeralda*, the heaviest, best-armed man-of-war on the Pacific coast of America. This he did with extraordinary success, at the risk of his life; and he brought the *Esmeralda* back to Valparaiso. He was much flattered and caressed, but later he was treated very shabbily indeed: his men were not paid, they were denied their

* Facsimile pages *MS I, 3a* and *4* mostly overlap. See O'Brian's note in the margin of *MS I, 3a*

7

prize-money from various sources, and upon some pretext his ship was threatened with impoundment. Yet though Jack sometimes behaved like a simpleton by land, and though he was often swindled ashore, he was sea-wise, and having provisioned and stored his ship with the basic supplies needed to carry her at least to some port in the Argentine, he handed the Chileans an ultimatum: either his men must have their due by a given date or he should sail away. They were not paid, and he did sail away. Yet although the *Surprise*'s voyage had something of the appearance of a failure, in fact the Spanish hold on South America was broken: and although this had not been the Admiralty's direct order, the result gave immense satisfaction in the proper quarters.

Furthermore Jack had on board a singularly amiable and gifted young man, the unacknowledged but much beloved illegitimate son of Prince William, Admiral the Duke of Clarence, a zealous sailor and almost certain to be king after his brother's death. Clarence had a great respect for Captain Aubrey (some of Jack's actions were indeed extraordinarily brilliant), and through Dr Maturin, who had treated His Highness for a variety of disease, mostly discreditable, had begged Jack to take the youth on this voyage: and young Hanson had distinguished himself as much as any loving naval father could have wished, cutting the *Esmeralda*'s cable and carrying her out under fire. Yet even this was not all: on the Pacific coast Jack and Stephen had met with a small stout vessel filled with fellow members of the Royal Society, two of whom, ornithologists, were determined to cross the narrow isthmus of Panama and return to London by the Atlantic. And these excellent creatures agreed to take Jack's dispatches – the news of his famous victory and the preservation of Chile – back to the Admiralty, then in the process of forming a South African squadron. Maturin and his chief, the head of Naval Intelligence, had long since established a system of rapid communication across the Andes, and it was thanks to this arrangement that Jack received the Admiralty's beautiful reply, a signal requiring him 'to proceed to the River Plate, there to go aboard HMS *Suffolk* taking command of her and hoisting his flag, blue at the mizzen,' that had spread such happiness throughout the ship.

Yet although the ephemeral Chilean ministry had fallen, to be replaced by one of its many rivals, the satisfaction that might have been supposed to accompany an assured independence was by no means general: there were many Chileans who regretted their old friends and their declared policies. Furthermore the feeling was not confined to Chile: there were many Chilean refugees and many of their Argentinian friends who had resented the Englishmen's presence and who now even more bitterly resented their absence – to say nothing of those many, many Argentinians who so clearly remembered the British capture of Buenos Aires and the even greater number of those who looked upon them as heretics, given to cursing the Holy Father almost every day.

Both Maturin and Jacob had caught wind of this feeling both in Chile and during their very beautiful passage of the Strait; and in the afternoon before they

MS I, 6

9

were to put in to San Pedro, a small sealing and fishing port at the bottom of an inlet on the northern shore with some sheltered arable land behind it famous for potatoes and cabbages on the one hand and prodigious mussels and crayfish on the other, Stephen said, 'My dear Jack, in the backwoods of America they say that an evil reputation is like an inextinguishable debt; and we have been so maligned on the Pacific coast that it might be prudent to arm the boats, or even to hale the ship so close to the strand that your great guns command the whole settlement.'

In the event the few inhabitants of San Pedro did not offer to challenge a reasonably powerful man-of-war moored broadside-on before their settlement, nor the powerful, cutlass-bearing seamen who walked along the quay. Yet although most of the citizens were at least partly Tierra del Fuegians and although none of them could have had any first-hand knowledge of recent events they were sullen and unfriendly, yielding only a few indifferent potatoes and wilted cabbages at an exorbitant price. However, the ship did top up her water from a clear free-running stream, no great distance from its parent glacier; and still with this blessed westerly breeze she pursued her long twisting course through the strait, Jack, Hanson and Daniel perpetually taking bearings, soundings, views of the shore (icy to the southwards, often raining to the north) and establishing a truly remarkable chart.

Stephen, who had no abilities whatsoever in this direction, confined himself to his medical duties of course (slight though they were, with a healthy crew and such an able assistant as Jacob), to watching and sometimes dissecting the birds, mammals and marine plants and creatures of the strait, and much of this he added to his letter to Christine, she being the only woman of his acquaintance who knew the difference between a jackass penguin and a macaroni and who delighted in the knowledge. She would also delight in the knowledge, reflected her lover, that these most inhospitable shores, often snowy on the south of the strait, always icy on the northern height, nevertheless sheltered at least one parrot or parakeet, a green bird with a fine red tail that flew in noisy groups in the beech-woods, and a minute humming-bird that could be seen sipping nectar from the fuchsias in Tierra del Fuego when the ship was on that side of the channel. He was reasonably well engaged with this letter one afternoon after dinner when Jack, abandoning his fiddle, returned to his surveying, and Stephen, closing his passage on Port Egmont hens (often to be seen), lifted his head to Hanson's reiterated 'Sir, if you please.'

MS I, 7

'Why, Master dear' – for Horatio Hanson was acting-master of the ship – 'I fear you have been waiting. I never heard you.'

'Not at all, sir: it was only that Dr Jacob feared you might have overlooked your appointment.' At this moment a tiny chime could be heard in the bosom of both, for each possessed wonderfully accurate repeating watches, the one a replacement of the minute timepiece that Stephen had given to Christine, the other Prince William's parting gift to his son. 'God love us all, and may I be forgiven,' cried Stephen, leaping up. 'It is half three – I am late.'

11

'Mind your step, sir,' said Hanson, steadying him. 'It is blowing up uncommon stiff from the west-north-west – has veered three points in half an hour, and *Ringle* is reefing hard.'

They made their way forward to the fairly well-lit and now vacant space in the sick-berth which the surgeons reserved for anatomizing – for the past few days they had been busy on a singular, probably undescribed dolphin; and as they carefully pared away, separated and described the muscular parts so they gave them to the cook's mates, standing there with buckets. The bones they kept for themselves. But today they had been obliged to stop. The frigate's motion was too great, and in spite of their skill and care their cutting was by no means accurate with the deck so very much awash.

'We are making ready to lie to, sir,' said Hanson in his ear. 'And the Captain says he will pass the word when it is fit for you to come on deck. In the mean time he desires you and Dr Jacob will stand by to deal with casualties.'

The first, to his own infinite shame, was Harding, the senior lieutenant – a straightforward fibula and tibia, which they very soon splinted and bound up: then came the usual series of bumps and bruises, diminishing as the furious gust blew itself out and ending with the Captain's compliments brought by Awkward Davies, and if now they chose to come on deck they would see 'a sight like a madhouse's washing-day – God love us – what rigging we have is fair stuffed, *stuffed*, with fucking poll-parrots and God knows what. Which I am to bring you up and cop three hundred lashes if you fall.'

MS I, 8

Stephen had of course heard of the South American parrots and he had often seen their little troops, but only from a distance, identifiable from their manner of flight and from their brilliant colour, so very unlike the general drabness of the Strait; and so eager was he to reach the first, entangled in the leeward shrouds, that he would certainly have gone over the side but for Davies' powerful restraining hand. And it was not only parakeets, though they of course were the most obvious and the most eagerly coveted by hands, who were perfectly accustomed to the African race: even more spectacular and even more wounding were the many kinds of minute birds, including Stephen's Tierra del Fuegian honey-sucker, that had been dashed against the rigging or the remaining sails with such force that in spite of their lightness they were quite shattered and as the blast died away, deck, lighter rigging and scuppers were jewelled all over with their pitiful but still brilliant fragments. Some of the more solid birds, particularly the parakeets and some red-crested woodpeckers, could be revived and patched to some degree, but upon the whole it was a most dispiriting task, the more so since there was very little hope of identification in most cases. Still Stephen, seconded by his mate, did what they could in the way of retrieval, mostly of skins (exceptionally difficult on that scale) and tiny bones: they took quantities of notes and they did a little something to increase their knowledge of this almost untouched avifauna.

For two and even three days after that furious blast the waters of the Strait remained strikingly turbulent, particularly in the Narrows, and great beds of kelp, torn loose from their basis, floated on every hand, sometimes endangering the rudder, sometimes checking the ship's way, and always disturbing birds, cetaceans and ordinary level-headed fishes. Nevertheless in spite of kelp, unexpected currents and strange vagaries of tide off a number of headlands, the ship's whole passage of the Strait, before she turned north, well out in the full Atlantic, with the Cape of the Eleven Thousand Virgins broad on larboard bow, lasted only three hours more than nine days.

'We are making pretty good time,' said Jack, 'and I think we may look into Port Desire and Bahia Blanca without keeping the Admiral waiting. He was not to sail till the twelfth.'

'Would you ever tell me, has he a numerous fleet?'

'Pretty considerable: three squadrons, of which ours, the blue, is of course the smallest – but, Stephen, do not think for a moment that I complain. Of course it is the smallest, being blue. But had it been half the size, I should still have given my right hand for it. Good Lord above: a flag at last! It was amazingly kind of them. Do not think for a moment that I complain, dear Stephen.'

MS I, 9

'It had not occurred to me at all, at all,' said Stephen. And he went on, 'Since my ill-bred questioning is so prosperous – and to be sure it is very ill-bred indeed – may I ask why you mean to stop at these South American ports, when I understood you to say we could sail home with what was in the hold?'

'Why, for fresh water and meat, of course, to say nothing of vegetables and fruit. We could probably

14

have got home, of course, but verminous, half-starved and rotten with scurvy: but that would have been a desperate stroke, in a God-damned desperate situation, one that a man could not stand. But now the case is altered. I am to join Lord Leyton in the River Plate, and I make no doubt – for he is a very active officer, as I know full well – that he will take the fleet down and across to the Cape with the utmost dispatch, and I prefer to be ready to weigh at the first hint of a signal, with the last cask of biscuit aboard and a well-fed, active, healthy crew – no shore-leave will be allowed.'

'But, my dear, *Surprise* is to go home, as you very well know, with your dispatches and all our letters home; and once there she reverts to the station of a private ship. Ever since we left Magellan's Strait and steered north the people have become increasingly aware of this, and the joy that filled the *Surprise* has sensibly diminished day by day. You know how unhappy our men from Shelmerston were when they were paid off with the peace and how wonderfully they revived when you took them aboard.'

'Certainly I know it very well, and I am going to use all what influence I may have to ease her back into the service. The squadron is pitifully short of frigates, and since I understand that our duty down there is the protection of the Indian and Chinese trade, nothing could be more useful than a nimble weatherly ship like *Surprise*. And I beg you will do the same. But even if we cannot succeed directly, I am allowed my bargemen and a good many other followers – I have little doubt that I shall house a score or so of the rest among my friends. And for those that are left, if there *are* any left, merchant shipping has revived wonderfully, and a seaman with a good character from the Royal Navy will not wait long for a berth.'

Just as it had been Hanson who first sighted Cape Pilar on their eastward leg, at the very opening of the Strait, so it was his particular friend Daniel who, spending his watch below in the foretopgallant crosstrees, caught the leading-mark for Port Desire in his glass, checked it twice, and called, 'On deck, there. On deck: St Paul's Rock, twelve to fifteen miles on the larboard bow. Dim. Comes and goes.'

MS I, 10

It came and went because of a heavy sea inshore that covered it entirely from time to time, if not with green water then with foam; and although the rollers moderated somewhat inshore, the frigate had an uneasy time, mooring in the sullen turbulences this side of the primitive mole-dirty water from some untimely flash-flood.

'I once saw a rhea here, some way inland,' observed Stephen, as he and Jacob were walking along the mean street (obscurely strewn with drowned dogs) to speak to the port-captain about water and vegetables. 'The South American ostrich, somewhat smaller than the African bird – a most inferior creature.'

'Ah?' said Jacob: and then 'I believe this must be the captain's house.'

The port-captain half rose when they came in, but he was far from cordial and he said that he could not recommend the town water after this diabolic flood and all the nastiness it brought.

Stephen spoke about the country inland, a hacienda he had visited, the kindness of the people. He and the others were of course speaking Spanish and after a while the port-captain said that there happened to be a clean spring at no great distance, but they would have to pay the proprietor a fee. 'It is not for myself, you understand. For my own part I am astonishingly generous, generous to a fault, even lavish . . .' He spoke of his faults at some length and then, having called for coffee, he asked in a confidential, almost affectionate tone, 'Why they, obviously old and rancid Christians, consorted with those vile heretics?' And when Stephen made the usual gesture of extreme poverty, rubbing thumb over knuckle, the captain shook his head, saying 'Ah, when the Devil drives . . . I shall send my boy with your men to Anita's spring, but they must be very respectful to her, and pluck off their hats. Her sister, Helena, the werewolf, will provide cabbages.'

So she did, fine upstanding plants, but without the least appearance of pleasure or (perhaps understandably) of common humanity: and both in these transactions and in a few others along the edge of the market the Surprises noticed a sullenness, a strong inclination to stare, muttering; while after some of their transactions the sellers could be seen to wash the coins or rub them industriously in the grit underfoot. Even if the *Surprise*, with her singularly fine lines and her thirty-six-gun frigate's towering mainmast, had not been so recognizable to a sailor's eye, her ensign would have identified her almost anywhere in the world, for on reverting to her function as a

MS I, 11

17

surveying-vessel under Admiralty command she had also reverted to the white ensign. At Bahia Blanca, their next port of call, Stephen, who was the natural emissary on such occasions, reported the same sullen apathy, not unmingled with a reluctance to sell, exorbitant prices and injurious expressions.

'Brother, you are playing at least half a tone too high,' said Jack that evening as they sawed away after an early supper.

'Am I?' cried Stephen, looking attentively at his fingers and twanging the string. 'So I am. I do beg your pardon. It is the shrill bitterness of my soul that makes its way out, I fear.'

'I am so sorry to impose these odious duties upon you, Stephen – pray take a sup of port – but you know, of course you know only too well, that when you and all your people have been without long enough you will descend to the basest means to relieve your wants.'

'I am not sure that the response is altogether civil: but be that as it may, I will tell you, Jack, that if they are bad in Port Desire and worse in Bahia, they are likely to be downright outrageous in the River Plate, where we are to meet the South African ships. Yet if I am not mistaken we are likely to be there well before Lord Leyton – well before even your little squadron . . .'

'What the Devil do you mean by *my little squadron*? It is a perfectly normal squadron, rather large than otherwise. Two ships of the line apart from *Suffolk*: a fifty-gun ship, two considerable sloops of war . . .'

'Hush, hush, Jack. Never fly into a passion, soul,' cried Stephen, seeing that his friend was seriously annoyed. 'Sure you must know after all this time that we use *little* as an endearment – a meliorative term, as one says my *little Puss* to a handsome Amazon that weighs fifteen stone in her shift. So we arrive, do you follow me now, well before his lordship, whom God preserve, and our natural allies, all because of our commendable zeal. Now let me beg you, for all love, to moor your ship close in against the southern shore for so much as an egg, an egg: for in a considerable city fanaticism can swell to a most surprising and horrible extent.'

At the end of the particularly grave adagio Jack put down his bow and said, 'Should you dislike it very much if we were to leave Bahia out of our plans? Our water and the cabbages have held out uncommon well and I had as soon push on quietly, if you understand me, to the River Plate, where there is a great resort of merchantmen and all sort of people that supply their needs, chandlers, smiths and the like: you are not dependent on the local werewolf. Not that I have anything to say against werewolves: the gentlewoman was perfectly civil, and her cabbages have stood up admirably.'

'I should not dislike it at all. Bahia has by all accounts some tolerable strands, but nothing in the way of lakes or marshland within striking distance: Jacob and I have an immense amount of sorting, reconstituting, classifying and preserving to do, and I had as soon sail on northwards – quietly, as you put it so well, quietly putting our collections in order.'

Quietly indeed they sailed along, with gentle breezes that wafted them generally northwards at something in the nature of five miles in the hour, northwards to even warmer seas. Little activity was called for, apart from the nice adjustment of the sails, and although the exact routine of the ship was never relaxed nor her very strict rules of cleanliness, these long sunny days with a soldier's wind seemed to many the ideal of a seaman's life – regular, steady, traditional meals with the exact allowance of grog; hornpipes in the last dogwatch, the deep melody of the Doctor's 'cello from the cabin and the cheerful sound of the gunroom's dinner; the future lost in a haze somewhere north of the equator.

So the golden days went by, and Stephen's mound of tiny skins mounted up, very carefully dried and treated against mites, against the voracious cockroaches that no amount of sulphurous fumigation could eliminate from the ultimate depths of the hold, their survivors breeding with extraordinary rapidity.

MS I, 13

By the time they were in flying-fish water again, the *Surprise* and her people had settled down to this very agreeable form of life – some few cases of sunburn and alleged moon-pall by night, to occupy Poll Skeeping and Maggie, and a series of quite deep, painful wounds or rather hook-billed bites from those parakeets that did not choose to be tamed; but for once, for *once*, no steady dosing for the pox. With a perfectly competent, conscientious, but by no means tyrannical first lieutenant, Jack Aubrey and his clerk could devote their hours to gathering all the scattered surveying material from the various notebooks and journals and cast it into the regular form most valued by the Hydrographical Department.

They were quite near the end of their work on the immense south Pacific crescent, at the northern tip of the Chonos Archipelago, which Jack had surveyed in freezing drizzle with a team of zealous and remarkably amiable young Chilean officer-cadets when the expected news came below. With the Master's duty, Mr Wells begged to tell Captain Aubrey that the leading-marks for the River Plate were clear from the mast-head, almost due north-north-west.

They were clearer still by the last dogwatch, when the declining sun lit them from behind; and in the morning the *Surprise* was well into the whole vast bay. All day long, with a gently favouring breeze they sailed up it until both shores could clearly be seen, and a fair amount of shipping: but never a sign of a man-of-war.

Farther, farther, with no more than her foretopsail now: a pause for dinner; and drinking his coffee on deck afterwards Jack said to Stephen, 'May I ask you and Dr Jacob to run up to the island with Wantage and make sure that our salute will be returned? This reception is so very curious that I should like to make quite certain. Mr Harding, please be so good as to have the blue cutter put over the side.'

The island was the chief of the many administrative centres: it was from the battery high on the seaward cliff that salutes were answered; and usually the place was like a fairly busy hive, with customs, quarantine and har-bour-dues officials swarming all over it, together with soldiers, sailors, marines and those grave gentlemen in long black coats, black-scabbarded swords, black neck-cloths and black wigs who were said to be very high in the administration. At present the place was singularly quiet, almost motionless, and since a salute was rarely returned without a good deal of bustle, the silence made all hands uneasy. It was known throughout the service that an unreturned salute was practically a casus belli. In any event it was the gravest insult and one that put an end to all communication with the shore. And to fire a salute without assurance that it would be returned was strictly forbidden. The question did not often arise, but in this case the atmosphere was so uncommon that Jack did not intend to run the risk.

MS I, 14

Yet while the coxswain was summoning his boat's crew Harding said to Jack, 'Forgive me, sir, but I believe I see a craft clearing from the lee-side. Yes, sir,' lowering his glass, 'I think it is one of their medicoes and a couple of dirty mates.' He peered again. 'Yes: a dirty, ill-looking crew in a dirty, ill-looking craft.'

They did not improve on closer acquaintance: at fifty yards from the frigate's side a man stood up and bawled 'Quarantine.'

Harding had a ladder put over and the party's leader, wearing a black coat and a yellow wig, followed by a youth with an ink-horn, came aboard quite nimbly. 'Dr Quental,' said the man in a very loud voice. 'Health. Speak Portuguese?' Wantage, who was fluent in the language, made as though to answer, but Stephen checked him. 'I am the surgeon of this ship, sir,' he said in Latin. 'Dr Maturin, at your service. I do not have the pleasure of speaking Portuguese, but I should be happy to answer any questions you choose to ask in Latin. And so will my colleague, Dr Jacob.'

Dr Quental put as good a face on it as he could, and

with more ease than the company expected he repeated a list of disorders by class: '*Exanthematici? Critici? Phlogistici? Dolorosi? Quietales? Motorii? Suppressorii? Evacuatorii? Deformes? Vitia?*'

Stephen considered all these, one by one, shaking his head after due reflection and then inviting their guest to come and view what invalids the ship possessed.

Poll Skeeping and Maggie had had plenty of time: their few patients (all with mill strains or broken bones apart from one with raging toothache, to be dealt with tomorrow, when his particular friend the armourer had finished a powerful pair of forceps to his own satisfaction) were correctly rigid in their cots, washed pink, brushed and incapable of movement, almost of drawing breath, so tight-strained were the sheets. Dr Quental was much impressed, much gratified by a draught of rum, happy to accept the compliment of a neatly-cased French amputating saw, and perfectly willing to give *Surprise* a clean bill of health. He also stated that in his considered opinion the fort would not hesitate to answer the ship's salute with exactly the same number of guns; having sorted his Latin with some care while he finished his glass, he told Stephen that he was an anti-clerical, that he had nothing to do with the public burning of heretics, and that he dared say there were very good men everywhere: among Jews, for example, or blacks, or even worse.*

MS I, 15

* The manuscript breaks off here for several pages – see O'Brian's note on *MS I, 15* – and the narrative is continued in the typsescript.

'Sir,' said Wantage in Stephen's ear as the Rio boat pulled away, 'his mates that did not go below with the Doctor, told me there was a rare old rumpus in the town last night, when some people from a barque out of Boston, the Boston in the colonies, stood up at a vigil and said it was great nonsense to say you were allowed only one wife: one wife at a time. "Look at King Solomon," they said; and it was taken very much amiss. Then one of them called out that he did not give a fig for the Pope of Rome, and fighting broke out. They said five Protestant houses were set on fire, and it might be much worse tomorrow, with the arrival of the Legate.'

'What's a legate?' asked Jack, when Stephen told him of this.

'In England they were usually called nuncios,' said Stephen: but in answer to a very severe look he added; 'An ambassador, as you might say – often plenipotentiary.'

'Well, I hope the silly villains have got it wrong,' said Jack with a look of strong dissatisfaction. 'This is the very last moment to become religious and start looking for stakes, gunpowder and – what do you call those things?'

'Sanbenitos.'

'Just so: sanbenitos. All we want to do is to fill up our water, buy a few fresh provisions and no doubt some wholesome fruit – we do not want to be racked, scourged and burnt: we get plenty of that at sea, free, gratis and for nothing – and pay our compliment to the Governor. Oh, that *Suffolk* would come in, followed by the rest of the blue squadron, then by Lord

24

Leyton with his ships and hey for Cape Town with never a papist in sight for the next ten thousand miles . . . I beg pardon, dear Stephen,' he added, looking earnestly into Stephen's face. 'I really did not mean to be unkind or personal.'

'I am sure you did not, my dear,' said Stephen. 'Pray when do you mean to start the salute?'

'Just as soon as the gunner tells the officer of the watch that all is right and ready, oh; and the officer of the watch tells Harding to his astonishment that we are all ready. Then, when I have begged Harding to proceed we shall, with luck, hear that fine measured boom, boom, boom. Twelve guns is usual for Rio, and I know that Harding is having the irons heated; for, do you see, with a red-hot iron in your touch-hole you cannot miss fire and have one of those embarrassing pauses in the solemn round. He is as eager as I am to have the barky as trim as the Royal yacht on occasions like this.

The day itself was by no means as trim as it would have been, but for the Legate's visitation; yet even so, at tea-time Killick came in, followed by Grimble, a procession of two, bearing the tea-tray (a great Spanish salver captured long ago) and a reasonable amount of anchovy toast, tea-cakes and a noble muffin.

Jack took tea seriously, as well he might, being so much exposed to the elements; indeed, he finished the two-men's muffin single handed; and then, wiping his buttery fingers, he directed an intelligent, almost a political look at Stephen, paused for a while, and then said, in substance, exactly what Stephen had expected him to say. 'There are, as you know better than I – far better, indeed, a good many of our people are . . .' Here he hesitated trying to find which was least offensive: Papists? Romans? Mumbo-Jumbo certainly would not do. *People of the old faith* sounded obsequious. 'Most of them are Irish, of course; though quite a few come from the English north country. And then there are the mere foreigners . . . that is to say, the foreigners.'

'There is something to be said for the word Catholics. It is in general use in Ireland.'

'Just so: thank you, Stephen. Well, in strange towns you quite often lead your band to a place where they hear what they expect to hear – a place where they are quite at home.'

'Just so. And, if you recall, I nearly always bring them back to the ship sober.'

'Indeed you do: thoughtful, contemplative and, as you say, dead sober. Now it just happened to cross my mind that was you to take them all to the cathedral, where I have no doubt the Legate will be pontificating, as is but right and proper, and if they were to be perfectly neat, fit to pass an Admiral's inspection, most uncommon solemn and pious, if you understand me, and was they to sing out good and hearty in the right places, it might tend to create a good impression, and persuade his Holiness that we were not all a band of gin-sodden raparees, given over entirely to whoredom and things I do not like even to mention. I hope you do not find my suggestion offensive, Stephen? For it is only a suggestion, do you see, not in any sense an order.'

'A very good suggestion, too. And I shall pass the word about my fellow-papists, letting them know, among other things, that it is for the honour of the ship that we should not all be blacked with a whole number of brushes – Lutherans, bigots, church-burners, destroyers of monasteries, sodomites and a number of other words that will instantly occur to your mind. But first, with your permission I will go ashore and gather what information I can: at present I swim in a sea of unknowing. The only thing that is at all clear is that upon the whole the people here do not love us as much as they should.'

What he said was quite true. Neither the British seamen nor the Royal Navy seemed really popular. Quite early in the morning a large scow, filled with much of the city's night-soil, heaved its massy burden overboard so close to the frigate's side that her paint-work was horribly fouled and her yardarms much endangered: all this to the cry 'Filthy sods,' which the Portuguese had obviously learnt from a merchant-man and which they repeated with unflagging zeal for a very long time, stopping only when some face-tious hands from an incoming trawler started throw-ing their more putrid cargo on to *Surprise*'s deck. The trawler, curiously enough, was garlanded if not with roses, then at least with some bright pink tropical flowers. Nor was she alone in this: very considerable numbers of other fishing-craft, from whalers down to one-rod tunny-men, came swarming up the bay.

During a pause in the hoots, the pelting and the obscene gestures, Stephen and Jacob returned, unhurt, unmolested, undefiled – they did indeed look very like foreigners, poor souls. They asked Jack to come below, and in the cabin Stephen said, 'Sir, I shall

speak for us both, if I may, although Dr Jacob's information is of greater value than mine and his connexions far more varied. In the very first place the
extreme clerical what I might call right wing element
means to overthrow the governor and the government
tonight or tomorrow. The Legate, who has great influence with the very large service population and above
all with their leaders is here to prevent or at least to
soften this movement: the ultra-clericals have little in
the way of armed support, and that is one of the reasons why they have made so much of this alleged
Protestant business, and why we were pelted with
dung. May I say how extraordinarily wise you have
been not to retaliate? To continue: this is the day upon
which the fishing-boats are blessed, a very considerable feast indeed, a holiday of obligation.' He looked
at his watch. 'I shall not go on prating any longer, but
let me beg you to come on deck now, with your glass:
and if necessary to go into the top to see the Legate
arrive at the top of the steps from which he blesses the
fishermen and their craft.'

Jack Aubrey did exactly what he was asked to do,
giving Jacob a hand at the last stage; and there they
stood all three, gazing out to starboard at the far, but
not so very far, side of the harbour, where a noble
flight of stairs led down to the water. At the side of
the step stood soldiers in scarlet cloaks; and on the
water the boat's kedges dropped, sails stowed, floated
quietly for their blessing. Suddenly the prodigious,
all-pervading sound of the vast crowd dropped to
something not far from silence, instantly filled by the
glorious sound of trumpets; and as the Legate, a fine

tall upright figure in a white gown, advanced to the head of the steps, the people cheered to the very vault of the sky.

'By God, he's black,' said Jack Aubrey, and a moment later his face was contorted with emotion.

'He is very happy,' murmured Stephen. 'Presently he will come over.'

Presently was a strange word to use: but while it lasted the Legate blessed, marked boats by the score, by the hundred, with holy water; and finally after an immense thunder of drums he told the assembly that the ceremony had been accomplished: they might now sail with God: It was as much a dismissal as *Ita, missa est*; but although something like silence came down upon the bay almost no one moved. They stood watching the Legate's splendid barge as it pulled straight across to the *Surprise*. The Legate came up the side like a right seaman and hurried across the deck to his father. 'Dearest Sam, you have not changed,' said Jack as they clasped hands. Then Sam knelt and patted his father's feet, a gesture as natural as the sun.

Then Stephen led his men forward, and they all kissed the Legate's ring. 'We must go,' said Sam, lifting his ear to a distant bell. 'But, sir, may I beg for my supper tonight?'

'I shall look forward to it extremely,' said Jack, and he went below while he could still do so with a decent composure.

In the close-packed community that made up the crew of a man-of-war there was extremely little privacy: they ate, slept, washed, relieved themselves in

MS I, 17

public; in public they were flogged, unless they happened to be officers – and in that case a severe admonition was very soon made known throughout the ship. Each man and boy knew exactly what the others earned and how much the married men sent home. And although the officers sometimes had private means, and were sometimes unwilling to speak of them, they also had servants, who knew whether their masters were bearing hard up for Poverty Bay or spreading all canvas for Port Lavish itself. The paternity orders that had brought many hands aboard were the subject of often-repeated wit.

There were few Surprises therefore who were much astonished at the very strong resemblance between the Nuncio and his host. It was perfectly well known that the younger man was one of Mr Midshipman Aubrey's indiscretions when, as a long-legged youth, he had served on the South African station, and that the boy, brought up by Catholic missionaries in Mozambique, had presented himself to his father in the West Indies, bearing the present of a charm, a ju-ju, from his affectionate mother, that had kept Jack alive through some really desperate encounters. Killick was of course a fount and a reasonably honest fount of information, much of it derived from Barret Bonden, Jack's coxswain and valued friend until he was killed in battle, a source of much greater value.

From this general history, therefore, what newcomers there were in that long harbour-watch, learnt that the good fathers, having taught Sam his letters and a considerable amount of Latin – the English he picked up with no sort of trouble – destined him for the minor orders: for nothing more, because of his illegitimate birth. But Stephen Maturin who, though a bastard himself, was very well-connected, obtained a dispensation for the young man, to whom he was particularly attached: and Sam had risen very fast indeed. To be sure, he was unusually intelligent and exceptionally good-natured: but he was also very black, shining black. And this was a time when a strong current of opinion in the Church felt that the rapidly increasing black world should be given very much more attention. On the merely practical side, the very, very large number of black men and women, slaves or hired labourers, particularly in South America, must necessarily influence the balance of power in time. Father Panda, who was a natural-born linguist, had already done excellent work in Brazil; and now he was sent to the Argentine with greetings, and perhaps some good advice to those who were, or who were about to be, in power.

MS I, 18

Chapter Two

'My God, that was a damned good dinner,' said MS II, 1
Captain Aubrey, rather loud, as though he were
addressing the mast-head. He was not referring to his
own meal with Sam, though that had been a capital
feast in the naval style, ending with a truly sublime
spotted dog, one at each end of the table, and
improbable quantities of port. No: this was a physically far more gorgeous entertainment, a dinner given
by the Governor in honour of His Excellency the
Most Reverend Doctor Samuel Mputa (he had kept
his mother's name), Papal Nuncio to the Republic of
the Argentine, whose government he and his allies
had undoubtedly saved very recently indeed, when a
numerous body of influential moderates, together
with their black followers, had defected from those
who were about to break out into open rebellion, and
had betrayed their arsenals. It was a dinner of high
ceremony, served on gold plate of more than ordinary
magnificence, with some particularly valued dishes,
such as the River Plate lobster in a bitter chocolate
sauce, and seventy of the finest guinea-pigs ever
brought down from the mountains.

To be sure, it did lack something of the family
atmosphere that had hovered in the frigate's great

cabin, with every guest and servant aware of the relationship and wholly in favour of the young parson's seamanlike ways, to say nothing of his willingness to drink his wine. Here the connexion, though not unnoticed, was much less obvious, Jack being seated, not indeed below the salt, but very much nearer to it, then his son at the very top, on the Governor's right hand.

He uttered these fine ringing words addressed to the Nuncio, a little way below him, as he made his way cautiously down the palace steps, Killick and, absurdly, Awkward Davies hovering at no great distance – pitiless steps with no rail, very sharp edges, deep treads; and it was usual to make an inward promise of a fortnight's or even a month's pay to one's patron saint before embarking on them in the darkness.

There were only six steps to go under the high-held torches when a small fat boy thrust his way through the crowd and called out, 'Sir, oh sir, if you please! The squadron is in the gut, just stemming the tide.'

'Thank you, Mr Wells,' said Captain Aubrey; and craning his neck to peer in the direction of the gut he missed his step and fell into His Excellency's waiting arms. Davies' prodigious strength supported the double burden: they recovered their balance, and Jack, walking along quite steadily, said, 'Sam, I am so very happy. The squadron is down there in the gut, stemming the tide. Even with this breeze they will be moored here off the island by slack water, and you will see me go aboard, ha, ha, ha! Now cut along, there's a good fellow: you must get a decent night's sleep.' A decent night's sleep: there were not many people aboard the frigate who had the least expectation of such a thing. *Surprise* had three mastheads, and all were firmly occupied by the nimblest, most far-sighted young men on her books, quite irrespective of rank, and they called down every movement of their distant friends together with the even more portentous news of faintly discerned sails far down the immense estuary, conceivably the main squadron under the orders of the commander-in-chief, South African station, Lord Leyton. The *Surprise* and her tender *Ringle* would soon come under the very close, very knowing inspection of at least one senior flag-officer and of the less authoritative but sometimes even more wounding scrutiny of large numbers of officers and above all of ratings; and there was nobody aboard either of the vessels who wished his own to be mocked, fleered at or called a second-hand mud-scow. They wanted no advice on cleanliness, seamanlike appearance or the priddying of decks, no facetious observations about their attire; and even the watch below spent much of their precious sleeping-time beautifying themselves and the ship. Perhaps the most active was Killick: Captain Aubrey had served as a commodore, so he already possessed a rear-admiral's uniform: these garments had been a great source of joy to Killick, but an even greater source of anxiety – termites in Malaysia, a shameless wombat in New South Wales, while from south of the Horn to the trackless wastes of the pampas innumerable forms of vermin had gnawed or attempted to gnaw the superfine broadcloth or ruin the gold lace

35

with their squalid dejections. During this anxious night, with so many of his shipmates scouring piss-dales or polishing musket-cocks, begging valuable slush from the cook or (more fruitfully) from his mates to give the round-shot something of a gleam as they lay along in the garlands by the great guns – during this active time he sat in the remarkably well-lit space where the surgeons often dissected their specimens or skinned their birds, sat there with Jack's best, rarely-used sea-chest open before him, half its contents spread out on a piece of sailcloth. His face was as pale as it could be, and it expressed not only horror but anguish too: for this strong clear light showed that his zeal in earlier, darker times had robbed the cloth of all its bloom. In places it was threadbare; and the heap of clothes had something of the sad, abandoned air so evident in the second-hand barrows of Monmouth Street.

'Pass the word for Killick,' called a voice from the quarterdeck, and the cry was repeated until it echoed from the open chest itself. Automatically the steward obeyed. 'Sir,' he said faintly to the towering captain.

'Have you laid out my number one uniform?'

'Well, sir, in a manner of speaking,' said Killick. 'Which it ain't what you might call weathered very well.'

Jack had never seen his steward so deeply moved. 'Be damned to that,' he said. 'Every God-damned thing in that chest was frozen stiff week after week, off the Horn. Just look out my ribbon of the Bath, will you? It sets off an old coat very well.'

'Beg pardon, sir,' said the officer of the watch. '*Suffolk* is launching a boat.'

Very true. Her barge was lowered down in a commendable fashion and manned: her acting-captain took his place by the midshipman in the stern. They pulled across with a particular accuracy of stroke and the coxswain brought her kissing alongside with barely an impact.

Captain Simmons came aboard nimbly in spite of his packet of letters. He saluted the quarterdeck and said, 'Good morning, sir. I thought you would like these' – holding up the bundle – 'as soon as possible.'

MS II, 4

'Good morning, Simmons – a very good morning to you – how pleasant to see you again. You could not have judged better. We have had no news from home this many a day. Such a welcome packet: thank you very much indeed.'

'Not at all, sir. Do you choose to come back in *Suffolk*'s barge with your own coxswain?'

'Thank you, Simmons, but I think I shall shift my clothes, look through the chief of these papers and then come across at about four bells.'

At the fourth stroke he ran down to the sadly weather-beaten boat where his coxswain was already sitting in the bows with his precious burden – ran down looking very grave. The red ribbon of his order shone in the light as he came aboard the *Suffolk*, but his face was as grave as ever: this was a profoundly serious occasion and he scarcely smiled as Simmons presented his officers.

This ceremony over, he nodded to his coxswain, standing there by the mizzen, and said, 'Heave out the flag.'

The folded bundle soared aloft, followed with the utmost concentration by all hands: at exactly the right moment, the exact height to an inch, the coxswain snapped the tie and the rear-admiral's blue flag streamed out bravely in the wind, instantly greeted by the first of thirteen solemn guns, enormously loud, salutes from all the members of the blue squadron, distant cheering from *Surprise* and clouds of wheeling, discontented gulls.

'May I suggest a tour of the flagship, sir?' asked Simmons, with what cheerfulness he could muster; and together they paced along the decks, through the heady scent of powder, watched with discreet intensity by all who could decently do so and by some who could not. 'Tell me, Simmons,' said Jack as they left the main magazine, walking delicately, as well they might with so many tons of gunpowder just behind them, 'does the Admiral sail with a flag-captain?'

MS II, 5

'He did,' said Simmons, embarrassed. 'But Captain Fielding is going home with me if *Surprise* can find room for us both.'

'Ah,' said Jack, aware that his question was untimely. 'I only asked because I thought he might answer some of my less important questions – an admiral has plenty to do without being pestered. Perhaps I might turn to his secretary.'

'I am afraid that would scarcely answer. Poor Coulter had been hauled over the coals before now for exceeding his office . . . it is very like what you and I knew aboard *Pegasus*.'

'Oh, indeed?' That had been a short, unhappy cruise when Jack was lent to the ship to take the place of her third lieutenant, shot through the head while attempting to board a Frenchman, *Pegasus* being a ship in which most people seemed to spend their time doing wrong. 'Is not *Suffolk* somewhat short-handed?' he asked, partly to change the subject but more to learn how a ship of the line could manage with so few people: the 'tween-decks were scarcely populated.

He did not learn, because the purser's clerk, an odd long-legged spectacled man devoured by curiosity, wished to find out who Captain Aubrey was, what he was doing here, and whether they would be able to water today or tomorrow – the great casks and hoses were all laid along – and as he uttered his almost mechanical questions, so he peered eagerly with his red-rimmed short-sighted eyes into Captain Aubrey's face, apparently devoid of shame. By the time his appetite, his very considerable appetite, was satisfied they had forgotten the shortage of hands and they walked on.

It was a long inspection and in the course of it Jack met almost all his new officers again, a seamanlike set of men on the whole, and cautiously welcoming – one or two former shipmates, known long ago. But he received a general impression of anxiety and over-work, an impression that was in part overlaid by his meeting with the gunner, the master-gunner, among his twenty-four-pounders, all as trim as heavy cannon could well be and all equipped with shining Douglas sights.

A long inspection, and by the end of it, when they stood there together in the bows, gazing out towards the approaching but still distant squadron Jack had come to like his anxious, somewhat hag-ridden companion well enough to ask, 'In really heavy weather, have you not found it difficult to work the ship with so small a company?'

'I have indeed: and I have heard of it, I do assure you . . .' He was cut short by a hail from the masthead and a moment later the message came forward: the rear-admiral was desired to go aboard the flag.

MS II, 6

'I am afraid it will be a wet pull,' said Simmons. 'May I lend you a tarpaulin jacket?'

'If you please,' said Jack: his fine but aged uniform had not much wear left in it and he was a long, long way from home.

A wet pull it was, through an increasingly choppy sea, right into the eye of the wind: it was however shortened by the zeal of the white and blue squadrons to reach a hospitable port.

'Well, Aubrey,' said the Admiral, looking at him with a certain satisfaction, 'You have had a wet time of it, I see. You should have put on an oilskin: still, we cannot all be wise all the time. I have called you out so far from shore because there are two questions I should like to settle. The first is supplies. We are very low in everything – tobacco is quite gone – and all the way down my pursers, agents and so on have had the utmost difficulty with the locals, even in ports where we have always been welcomed and entertained.

Difficulties about water, difficulties about cattle . . .
even about shore-leave and common supplies – no
bumboats coming off, no whores. What is it like with
you in Buenos Aires? Should I push on? Things are
desperate low and with the present ministry I dare not
use force. How are things with you?'

'My lord, until a few days ago we had great difficulty in getting supplies of any kind, but then an eminent ecclesiastic, a Papal Nuncio particularly well
known to my political adviser Dr Maturin . . .'

'Yes, yes. Sr Joseph mentioned him to me: I shall
pay him some attention.'

'. . . came in and now everything is settled. We lack
for nothing, and prices are very moderate. We are
amply stored for the Cape, and *Surprise*, which is now
bound for home with my dispatches, is in much the
same case.'

'I am heartily glad to hear of it. That will be a very
great relief.' Lord Leyton uttered these words, but his
aged yellow face did not match them at all. His
expression remained discontented, querulous, ready
to find fault or to contradict. However he did say,
'*Surprise*: yes, that reminds me. One of the reasons
that I asked you to come out was to tell you that I
intend to send two of my officers home in her and to
ensure that there should be no trouble about taking
them and an unsatisfactory midshipman aboard your
vessel.'

MS II, 7

'You will forgive me, my lord, but *Surprise* is no
longer my vessel. To be sure, I did command her, but
she was on hire to the Hydrographical Department of
the Admiralty until I should meet your squadron,

hoist my flag and take up my new appointment. The moment I did that, *Surprise*'s contract with the Admiralty came to an end. She returns to the sole ownership of her proprietor, a free agent. If you wish I will ask him whether he chooses to take these people aboard: but it is entirely at his discretion. He is at no man's command.'

'What a damned hair-splitting sea-lawyer you are, upon my word, Aubrey,' cried the Admiral. 'You can damned well go back to that half-baked privateerly donkey-frigate and give the owner my orders to take these two officers and the reefer aboard. If he makes the slightest demur or objection tell him that I shall press every man in his ship and leave him to wallow in the mud of the River Plate until she rots.' At this point the Admiral's yellow face had a curious flush and his eyes fairly blazed: one clenched fist rose and fell.

'*The slightest demur or objection . . . shall press every man . . .*' repeated Jack, rising and drawing his tarpaulin round him.

'Awkward, legalistic, cavilling sod . . .' muttered the Admiral: and then, more audibly, as he rang for his steward, 'Sit down, sit down, and drink some madeira to the squadron's supplies. Amphlett' – to the steward – 'the decanter of madeira from the coach: and a couple of glasses.' A pause, and he went on, 'I do not like to ask a political adviser to come out in this blow – the doctor physicked Prince William, did he not? I am told he is very well with His Highness. But if you would tell him that you have explained the situation and that I should take it as a personal favour if he would allow these people to go aboard his ship, I should be obliged to you.'

'Very good, sir. Now if I may I shall carry your message to Dr Maturin: if I were to take your purser and perhaps your secretary back with me to *Surprise*, my people could tell them all we know about our plentiful, *plentiful* sources of supply. The present governor is entirely on our side, and I do not think you will be disappointed.'

'Make it so, Aubrey,' said the Admiral, rising. 'And when you dine aboard me tomorrow, pray bring your political adviser. I should be happy to be acquainted with him and to offer what civilities I can. I presume he goes home in *Surprise?*'

'I cannot tell, my lord: his mission in Chile is clearly at an end – a most satisfactory end – but there may also be some duties waiting for him in South Africa and above all eastwards. He and Dr Jacob are very knowing about those parts. But in any case I mean to return to her at once, and transfer some of her hands to poor thin *Suffolk.*'

'Aye. It was the yellow jack. Off Port of Spain.'

'And I shall carry your message. Your servant, my lord, and thank you for the capital madeira.'

The pull back had the breeze and the sea right aft, and Jack went aboard *Surprise* in fine style, the side dressed by smiling seamen and officers. He asked for the Doctor, who, unused to the ceremonies attending a flag-officer, was reading in the great cabin, reading his letters from home. Jack noticed his gravity but delivered Lord Leyton's invitation and said, 'I shall be back in a few minutes: please sort out my post and I shall join you.'

On deck he gave the not unexpected order for all hands and when the particularly attentive group was assembled he said, 'Shipmates, as you know, the barky is going home. Some people are uneasy in their minds at being thrown ashore in peace-time . . .' A general murmur of agreement: intense interest. 'Well, I can take sixty-three prime seamen over to *Suffolk* with me. Aboard her it would in course be the same pay, rations and allowances as here, and in her you would find some officers you already know and a score or two of former shipmates. So let them as choose to serve on the South African station ask my clerk to set their names down on a list and I shall mark those I think best suited for the climate.'

A general buzz of strong approval, not quite a cheer, out of respect for a flag-officer, and Rear-Admiral Aubrey plunged below, where Stephen looked up with a frown, pushing Jack's heap towards him and silently going on with his own.

MS II, 9 Sophie Aubrey had almost all the virtues of a woman who had had the meagre education of her class, taught by a singularly ignorant governess – little beyond the three R's and a smattering of French together with a list of good and bad kings. She had never been encouraged to read and in fact she had read very little; but she could and did write a singularly beautiful hand. Her piano-playing was purely mechanical, yet then again she had naturally pretty manners, she was tall and slim, her complexion was quite admirable and she moved with a perfect, unconscious

44

grace – it was a delight to see her going down the dance. But she was an indifferent, unwilling horse-woman in spite of arduous, dreaded lessons in her youth and her husband's kindly-meant encourage-ment: and she had never learnt to date her letters.

Jack's bundle had not come aboard arranged in order of time and although from a few hints thrown out by chance – gifts of partridges, the flowering of certain shrubs, children's holidays, birthday feasts – he slowly imposed a remote hint of sequence he could scarcely confide in it at all. He did make out that his valuable agent was managing his more dis-tant estate – the inherited rotten borough that gave him a seat in Parliament – remarkably well, that the Woolcombe land was more prosperous than ever it had been, and that generally speaking the children's health, apart from the usual coughs, colds and one greenstick fracture, was all that could be wished.

The pattern, the history of all that these many let-ters told, was still very far from clear, but the hint of discord and unhappiness that he had acquired from the first random pages and that he had carried with an anxious mind to the *Suffolk* – the hint that had much increased the gravity of that ceremony – now expanded to a conscious and reasoned certainty: there had indeed been grave unhappiness at Woolcombe, and in all likelihood the unhappiness was still there.

From time to time he glanced over at Stephen, who was equally grave, but whose letters – whose dated and indeed numbered letters (for from early childhood Christine had been brought up to keep

45

exact ornithological and botanical records) were now assembled in neatly-ordered piles that he was at present annotating in a private script, just as he would have annotated any other body of intelligence documents. From time to time Stephen felt his friend's gaze heavy upon him; but this was an exceedingly delicate affair, with very strong emotions involved, and he did not choose to broach a subject that concerned Jack even more than it concerned him: still less did he wish to force a confidence. He therefore made no observation of any kind until Jack turned and said, 'Brother, I am most uncommon stupid today, what with the emotion of hoisting my flag – hoisting my flag, God bless us all – and having a set-to with Lord Leyton as well as coping with our people – and I cannot make head or tail of what is afoot at home, except that they do not seem to be quite friends. Have you puzzled it out? I mean, if you have had the same kind of letters?'

'I believe I have, my dear, though I may well be mistaken. You will recall that Christine went down to Woolcombe at my particular request and at dear Sophie's invitation?'

'Yes, yes: I remember it perfectly.'

'At that time your twin daughters were away, at their aunt's school in Ulster.'

'Just so. They travelled with James Callaghan, whose eldest girl is there too.'

'So at Woolcombe there was just Sophie, your young George on long leave while his ship was refitting, Christine Wood and my Brigid. Edward Heatherleigh had brought them down from the North Country, but at that point he did not stay, having at least three papers to read before the Society.'

'All this while we were moving slowly down towards Brazil.'

Stephen nodded and went on, 'Perhaps I told you that among a quantity of letters that I received at Funchal there was a note from Edward speaking of his delight, in the countryside about Woolcombe and his hope of hunting there one day?'

'I believe you did. Do you think a pot of coffee would sharpen my wits?' He touched the bell. 'You will take a cup, I am sure?'

Stephen agreed and went on. 'That was the posture of affairs: a very elegant posture too, with George and Brigid excellent good friends, often riding on a stout well-boned pony – the source, alas, of that greenstick fracture.'

'It knit very soon and it earned him another three months' leave.'

'To be sure. And this was the state of affairs when Edward came back from London. He had been charmed by the reception of his papers and he was even more charmed by the countryside; he thought it ideal for fishing, for hunting fox or hare, and for *MS II, 11* recording the movements, mating, nesting and diet of an extraordinarily large number of birds, and he asserted that he should start making enquiries for a house to be let or sold, observing that although their place in the north was very well, the weather was exceptionally and increasingly severe, which his declining health could no longer endure. So Sophie, judging very rightly from his carriage, servants and evident style of living, suggested a comfortable, fair-sized house a quarter of a mile away.'

'Medenham.'

'Just so . . . which had been empty for some time, but which, with a gardens and meadows, had been carefully kept up and which was to be had at a modest rent by a tenant such as Mr Heatherleigh, and if dear Christine liked she would ask the agent for an order to view.'

The brother and sister viewed with every intention of being pleased and they came away delighted. Indeed they would have been difficult to satisfy if they had not liked Medenham, a warm, comfortable, spacious, low-built house of Charles II's time with linen-cupboards fit to shelter a troop of horses, massive furniture of another age and a considerable library, mostly of travel and natural philosophy.

The affair was soon concluded; necessaries and a few servants were sent down from the north, and the new tenants moved in; the nearby families soon paid their visits, and Mr Heatherleigh and his sister were pronounced a great acquisition to the neighbourhood, particularly as Mr Heatherleigh spoke eagerly of his intention to hunt that year.

This however proved a hope not easily realized. The horses were soon in the stalls, a handsome bay mare and two promising grey geldings, but Mr Heatherleigh had a troublesome neighbour in the north who coveted his estate and when it was refused to be sold this man turned to the exceedingly complex law governing mineral deposits in those parts which, he contended, gave him the right in the peculiar jurisdiction of the province to pursue an uninterrupted vein under the adjoining land – under Edward Heatherleigh's land. Before Michaelmas, therefore, the poor man climbed into his coach again and travelled northwards to his bitter moors through the driving rain, to spend all his diminishing energy in lawyers' meetings and vain *MS II, 12* attempts at understanding counsels' opinions on the most profoundly obscure customary laws of usage where minerals were concerned in that particular district.

During this period Christine spent much of her time at Woolcombe, and so, except for those necessary hours in the school-room with her new governess, the capable and intelligent Miss West, did Brigid, walking in and out as though it were her own home, often accompanied by her companion George, who sometimes improved his indifferent mathematics with Miss West and sometimes showed both governess and pupil the higher flights of knotting.

It was during the later part of this season when field mushrooms were to be had by the basketful for the picking that the little household began to look for the return of Mr Edward – he had uttered some general remarks about having a wheel retyred and the horses shod – when a carriage was heard coming up the drive. For a few moments those who were drinking tea in the small drawing-room thought it might possibly be Mr Edward's coach, sounding soft because of the rain: but not at all – it was a common post-chaise bringing the twins earlier than usual (not at all uncommon with Sophie's sister, who would seize upon any conveyance, any travelling-companion, to send her pupils home).

The letters that described this homecoming varied; but Stephen, who knew those concerned extremely well, saw the Aubrey girls hurrying in, tired, cross and hungry, intensely jealous at seeing Brigid sitting there by their mother, warm, prettily dressed and well-fed. 'Are you still here?' asked Charlotte. 'You are always here!' cried Fanny, and there was some motion towards pushing her off the sofa, strongly repelled by George. Clearly Sophie and Christine dealt with the situation – the clack and din of the accompanying County Armagh maidservant was a great help – and the Aubrey girls were taken away, washed and fed, while Christine led Brigid home, desiring Padeen to carry the twins' trunk indoors and settle with the postillion.

'As I see it, dear Jack,' said Stephen, 'the twins' jealousy, exacerbated by the weariness of travelling, extreme hunger and the hot squalor of a post-chaise, exploded into open violence when they saw Brigid there, brushed and in a handsome garment sitting in the most favoured place next to their mother. A good night's sleep, a body-bath of warm water, fresh clothes and a substantial breakfast is likely to restore all their amiability.'

'I am sure you are right,' said Jack, but he did not believe it. He knew, far better than Stephen, that there was little amiability to restore. Not from the beginning, when the little girls were virtually one being, but quite early, he had seen this jealousy directed by a mutual common understanding against any person, any creature even, for whom their gentle and affectionate mother showed a particular liking.

MS II, 13

50

Their father, being a sort of household god, was exempt, and so were some of the minor animals; but not George, who was accused of siding with Brigid against them and of running after her like a little dog.

It was an unhappy state of affairs, above all that Edward Heatherleigh was away in the north and that in his absence Christine was staying at Woolhampton, where her support for Brigid increased the atmosphere of ill-will.

'Sometimes I count the remaining days of holiday on the calendar,' write Sophie. 'They seem to stretch on and on, and I am so afraid that Christine and I may quarrel. Sometimes I see her check the angry words when the twins are particularly unkind: and rather than have that I am minded to suggest that she and Padeen should travel up to the north to stay with dear Edward, at least until the girls go back to school. I know that she is particularly anxious to escape the attentions, the very pronounced attentions, of Captain Miller.'

'I do not think I know about Captain Miller.' said Stephen. 'What is his ship?'

'Oh no: he is only a soldier,' said Jack. 'He has a moderate estate the other side of Caxley. A surprising number of pheasants; but a sad coxcomb, I fear. I only say 'How d'ye do?' when we meet. A soldier: his regiment was posted to Sierra Leone at one time. That will be the Admiral,' he said, breaking off as the salute *MS II, 14* began, doubled and redoubled by echoes and by the citadel's prodigious reply to Leyton's civility.

'The Admiral is at hand,' said Jack in the flattened silence, 'and I should have told you before that he

51

begs the favour of passage home for his flag-captain and another unfortunate whose name I forget. And I rather think, brother, that I have pledged your word in exchange for the moving of sixty-odd prime hands to *Suffolk*, which can hardly win her anchors else. Oh, they were so happy when . . .'

'Wittles is up,' said Killick, and the scent of toasted cheese wafted in with him.

They ate in silence, intently, hungrily; and then, resting his fork, Jack said, 'I have had what I think is an idea worthy of Newton: but during the night I must spend the rest of my time reading the rest of my letters and unless they contradict me I shall tell you at breakfast: for once that is eaten, *Surprise* must make sail.'

Chapter Three

The diminished but still well-manned *Surprise* and her lithe fore-and-aft companion *Ringle* swung easily at their moorings on the making tide not far from the imposing *Suffolk*, and they gazed at the South African squadron farther inshore, actively victualling, watering and getting ready to move into various docks and yards beyond the citadel for repairs, some of them urgent.

MS III, 1

'Good morning, Stephen,' said Jack as his friend walked into the cabin.

'Good morning to you, my dear,' said Stephen.

'You have done your writing, I see?'

'So I have too: a simple harsh direction that Brigid shall be delivered into the hands of the bearer and carried aboard – whichever vessel we decide upon – there to be in her father's custody: this is, as I understand it, a necessary legal form in case any of Diana's relatives should object. It is, I hope entirely softened by a most affectionate private note to Christine and her brother, inviting them to join us.'

'I have done much the same, simply requiring Sophie to come aboard with the utmost dispatch, bringing a minimum of impediments, and of course the girls.'

Each eyed the other's letter, which looked more like a laboured study than a simple note; and Jack said, 'Well, let us at least have a preliminary cup, and then we can ask Harding to join us.' Some moments later he touched the bell, and said to Killick, 'Ask Mr Harding to walk in. Mr Harding, pray sit down – may I pour you a cup of coffee? Now you know very well that *Surprise* and *Ringle* are to return to Portsmouth with all possible speed to deliver a certain number of officers to the Commander-in-Chief, together with the Doctor's communications and my dispatches. You may find it possible to shape your course without any impropriety so that you touch at Shelmerston before heading for Plymouth. If it is feasible, you, a firm-natured married man, will post straight to Woolcombe and there hand this letter to my wife and this to Mrs Wood, her near neighbour. Our hope, do you see, is to convey both ladies, together with Mrs Wood's brother,

the three children and the strict minimum of attendants to the Cape, either catching the squadron before it leaves the River Plate or joining company during the voyage – they will almost certainly water at Saint Helena – or simply at the Cape itself. Now you know both vessels through and through; and you know more than I do about children, attendants and the married state. When you have heard the ladies express their views on baggage and on these points you will form an opinion on the irreducible minimum and choose your conveyance accordingly. *Ringle* is undoubtedly faster than *Surprise*, but I should not like to have her passengers unduly cramped – given a disgust of the sea – for the sake of a few days.'

'Two ladies, one gentleman, three children, and I suppose three or four maids and a man.'

'It does of course depend on whether the gentleman chooses to come,' observed Jack. 'Mr Harding, you will read these letters if you please: they are in no way confidential.'

'I make no doubt that the gentleman will come,' said Stephen.

Harding, a poised middle-aged lieutenant, read the letters with attention. The others watched him. 'Well, sir,' he said at last, 'Well, gentlemen: I am of opinion that *Ringle* is the right choice. I was perpetually easing my sheet when she was in company with *Surprise*, though indeed there are few faster frigates. The passengers will not lie altogether at their ease, to be sure, but they will have the delight of seeing the bow-wave flung wide to leeward and the wake racing away, everything alive and tearing through the water. They would be dull souls that did not love that: and if I may be so bold, Miss Brigid loved it purely last time she was afloat in a blow. Anyhow, you would want *Ringle* as a tender, sir.'

'Very true: so you think all these people could be crammed in?'

'I should take my davy on it, sir.'

'Very well. You can sail with *Surprise*, then; and she will deliver my officers, passengers and despatches at Portsmouth, then run down to be laid up in Sepping's yard, while you return with your passengers in *Ringle*.

'Very good, sir,' said Harding, folding the letters away in his bosom. 'So now, since the gentlemen for

MS III, 3

Portsmouth are already aboard *Surprise*, I shall ask permission to take my leave and wish you and *Suffolk* a happy, prosperous voyage. And Doctor, how I hope you and your mate may bag a brace or two of phoenixes.'

They shook hands and parted. 'There is a fine fellow,' said Jack. 'He can sail the schooner very, very hard indeed: it was the right choice. But I think he was not mistaken when he said they would not always lie at their ease.'

'It would be ill-natured on my part to suggest that he might be influenced by the certainty, under Providence, of coming back to your blue squadron and acting as tender to the imposing great *Suffolk* under your command: I shall not say it however, although my lower being does feel exceptionally bad-tempered today. Jack, with your idea you have wholly forestalled me. You spoke of a notion worthy of Newton, but you did not elaborate: and I was only waiting for an opportunity of telling you mine.

'Pray do so now, dear Stephen: I am sure it would be more luminous.'

'What I was going to say was that you had no idea of the fundamental difference between a mere land-lubber and a seaman.'

'Oh was you, indeed?'

'You may toss your head in that superior way, but you have never been a *mere* landlubber. You were introduced to the ocean as an infant child; you boated before you knew the difference between right and wrong; you went positively to sea under Captain Willis well before puberty. Far from you the wondering

calf-like gaze of those who watch the intrepid
mariner traverse the tossing deck – the gaze almost
instantly followed by a feeling of unavoidable and
certain death, cold death, followed by furious uncontrollable heaves and shameless vomiting, morbid MS III, 4
frigor and despair. They, with some slight recovery
and even an upright position, the sight of these god-
like creatures stalking about the nightmare deck in
their uncouth garments, uttering their brutish cries,
haling upon ropes great and small – finding their way
by night – reaching the stated port – all this reduces
the lubber to a state of laudable and permanent
humility. No, no, my good sir, you may say what you
please, but there is a great gulf fixed between the
landlubber – the landlubber who comes late to
things that float – and the true-born seaman: a gulf as
great as that between a sheep and a seal.'

   'Very true,' said Jack, who had had the training of
some of the sheep.

   'Now you are to consider,' Stephen went on, 'that
my Brigid was not only baptized in sea-water, but
dipped before she could walk. When we were ashore
she rejoiced in boats, when we were afloat she
delighted in heavy sea, never minding in the least
when they soaked her through and through – nimble
in the rigging, the darling of the upper-yardmen. She
often explains the rigging to me, and I have seen old
hands like Tobin nod with approval. No, my dear
Jack, what I should have said had you not in essence
said it before me, was that one (however young) who
has sea-legs, sea-sense and a knowledge both acquired
and to some degree as it were instinctive of the sea's

very nature itself bears down all frippery land-based experience, however old.'

'Oh come, Stephen, Charlotte and what's her name are not exactly crones. As I remember they only date from the Mauritius campaign.'

'They might have been born with Helen of Troy as far as that is concerned. Aboard, particularly aboard so lithe and eager a vessel as *Ringle*, Brigid must bear them down; and a just equilibrium will be reached, with mutual respect and no bullying.'

MS III, 5 There were many vantage-points high above the harbour that Jack and Stephen used to climb, once a reasonable period had elapsed, a period in which a well-handled weatherly craft with favourable winds (and as far as could be told they had been favourable) could reasonably be expected to sail out and back; and Stephen had the pleasure of seeing some moderately upland birds and the bizarre mating habits of a colony of variegated scorpions, while the sun passed over the almost invariable translucent sky; but Jack always made his descent to the still fairly active yards (Lord Leyton's mainmast footing still gave great trouble) with hope disappointed.

By now *Suffolk* was in very fine fig, and since Jack was blessed with an experienced and upon the whole intelligent wardroom, the gun-crews, at least in dumb-show, were as brisk as he could wish while the small-arms men (who could, within limits, fire their pieces) were all well above the average. Her stores were completed – prime salt beef from the immense ranches, smaller amounts of moderate pork, a remarkably agreeable army biscuit, tobacco in industrial quantities – while for daily use flesh-boats plied to and from the butchers stalls along the quay, and flat-bottomed craft brought fruit and vegetables in unlimited amount. As a peace-maker the Nuncio had worked wonders, though to be sure commercial enterprise had played its part.

'It is only a Friday,' said Jack, when he and his first lieutenant (he sailed without a flag-captain) had made sure that there was not a becket out of place and that all Suffolks were present, correctly shaved and provided with all that was required. 'It is only a Friday, but I think I shall stroll up well beyond our usual mound with a telescope. Do you choose to come, Stephen?'

'I do, too: we might see some of the first migrants.'

Up and up: fairly easy going now that they were used to the land; and as they rose the horizon increased enormously, the empty horizon, though in with the land there were some lateen-rigged fishermen.

The mound they chose was thinly covered with a sparse herbage in which there grew a small particularly vicious cactus, while in the many bare places the earth showed dull purplish red: a landscape more wholly foreign they had never seen, although they had travelled very, very widely – it was, after all, their calling.

MS III, 6

'Dear Lord,' said Jack, sitting comfortably down, his back to a rock, after a piercing search of the nearer sea and the northern horizon, 'how I long for Woolcombe and the green Woolhampton downs, speckled with sheep. Woolcombe and the soft dew falling: the cawing of rooks. When I was a mere post-captain, you know, and there was this prospect of peace, I used to console myself, particularly when I was solvent again with that dear prize-money and Cousin Edward's land doing so well – I used to console myself with the thought of restoring the place to what it was when I was a boy, before my father lost his head about the Stock Exchange, when we had a pack of hounds and a damned good huntsman and when the water-bailiff kept the streams as neat as a man-of-war: full of trout and the odd salmon on the spring run. Lord, we had such sport, such fun! There was an old hound called Captain, and he always hit off the line after a check. "Hark to Captain" we would cry, and they all followed him like a single creature. Lord! How I longed to be back! Now of course I must stand my trick as a flag-officer: and most uncommon lucky I am to *have* it to do. But I do so long to be back, sometimes, under Hamble Down, showing George how to work out a line. Stephen, you can have no idea how beautiful it is.'

'Can I not?'

'Oh of course you can, of course you can. I am sure the Glens of Avoca are even finer. I do beg your pardon. But, do you see, it was *my* childhood.'

'Have you noticed that small vessel right in with the land, almost beneath us, under the cliff? Her sails are all in a line.'

Jack leapt to his feet. 'By God, she's *Ringle*,' he cried. 'She must have stood inshore . . .' The voice and the explanation died on the downward slope.

'I should never have believed that a man so tall and stout could have moved so fast,' murmured

Stephen, fixing the schooner in his glass. He liked to believe that he could make out Brigid and Christine with Edward Heatherleigh clinging to a spar behind them, but it was clearly time to descend.

The perilous slope, the milder slope, the mule-track, the paved road, and at last the quays with Jack still far, far ahead, though now moving more like an admiral.

Ringle was a beautifully-proportioned vessel and it was only when there was a tight knot of people on her fo'c'sle that one saw how small she was in fact. Kindly hands heaved on the mooring ropes to let Stephen step aboard from the quay, and clear over the general din he heard the Aubrey twins' shrill cry, raised for the seventh time, 'Why are you not wearing your admiral's uniform?' while at the same time his own Brigid slipped through the throng and whispered 'Dearest Papa' as he bent to kiss her. Christine was just behind, and looking up from the child's shining, happy, sun-browned face he said, 'Dear Christine, she does you infinite credit. Edward, my dear sir, how do you do? How happy I am to see you.'

The visitors' cabins had long since been prepared, and now the admiral's barge carried them over: after their extraordinarily rapid but somewhat cramped voyage they were amazed by the scale of a ship of the line. 'It is almost as good as Grignon's hotel,' said Charlotte, which earned her a sour look from Killick. 'And have you noticed that the sails are square?' asked her sister, to which Brigid replied, 'Don't you know the odds between a ship and a schooner?' with such firmness and such effect that

Stephen saw, with infinite satisfaction, that a decent balance had been established. Then again, Brigid knew quantities of old Surprises, some of whom had taught her the ropes: these she found out and asked them how they did, calling them by name, which put her head and shoulders above any passenger but Mrs Aubrey. In any case the twins never entered into competition: as might have been predicted, they had been dreadfully seasick, confined to their bunks, horrible to see and worse to hear from the very beginning until a few days ago, so that they had acquired no sea-legs, no fundamental knowledge; and even now they were incapable of distinguishing a bowline from a rolling-hitch.

MS III, 8

Yet in a surprisingly short time as it is measured by days the new inhabitants of the *Suffolk*, even the more stupid of the Aubrey girls, took bells for granted, the ritual swabbing of decks, set meals (less Spartan now that they lay in port) and the many and very fine gradations that separated the rear-admiral from the boy, third-class. Stephen observed, with a mute but intense satisfaction, that here his daughter had not the least air of being a stranger in the house, a friend's child accepted for that friend's sake: here, with so many friends and accompanied by Padeen, an old Surprise of remarkable standing and authority, she was very much at home. Yet as far as he could see she did not flaunt her sea-going knowledge, but as soon as the twins were willing to be peaceable she was both kind and companion-like.

Very soon they had explored almost every part of the ship from the safer tops (propelled by Padeen and other seamen) to the echoing vaults of the darkened hold, where facetious midshipmen and first class volunteers would terrify them with sepulchral moans and waving sheets.

'Dearest Stephen,' said Sophie, passing him a cup of tea in the cabin, 'I cannot tell you how glad I am that our daughters are friends again: there was a time when I almost despaired – when I should have whipped them if I had not thought it would do more harm than good. It only made me dogged when I was young.'

MS III, 9

'I cannot imagine you being whipped, Sophie,' said Christine.

'But I was, and quite often too. My mother would make us stand with our faces to the wall and whip the back of our legs with a thin sheaf of willow-wands: I do not think it ever improved my French verbs or arithmetic or even my manners.'

'I knew some Dominican nuns who did that,' said Stephen. 'They whipped my Saavedra cousins until they bled: I had thought it was only Catholic. Jack hardly ever flogs: discourages it, indeed. How do you find him, my dear?'

'Oh, very well, I thank you,' said Sophie, blushing. 'I must admit he is rather thinner than I could wish: but he does *love* having his flag, and I am so very, very happy for him. It was Prince William who sent us the news, with his best compliments, which I thought wonderfully polite.'

The three little girls came in, since if there was tea there might also, in the nature of things, be cake, or at least muffin. On seeing Stephen they stopped, not looking very wise, and made a concerted bob: then

Brigid ran over to him and said, 'Oh sir, the Admiral says a Portuguee came in with the flood and he hopes there may be some mail. A boat pulled across to the flag not long since.'

'I shall go upstairs – I shall go on deck, and ask whether it would be proper to enquire. Ladies, forgive me, I beg.'

No. It would be most improper. Jack was surprised that a man who had seen so much sea-time could suppose the thing possible or even decent – it was not exactly mutinous but it would deserve and certainly receive an exceptionally harsh reproach. But in any case Stephen was talking great nonsense. The Portuguese had been aboard Lord Leyton this hour and more and there had been no sign of mail – nothing handed up the side, no passing out of bags, no hurrying to and fro. No. The boat had done nothing more than deliver a gentleman, the gentleman in regimentals who was now walking up and down the quarterdeck with the Admiral, arm in arm. 'I have been staring at him with my glass, in this ill-bred fashion, for some little time,' said Jack. 'For although I think I know the face and carriage I cannot put a name to either. Should you like to take a look?'

'Sure, it is very ill-bred: but I might, to make you easy.' Stephen took the telescope, focused it, and almost at once, as the two men on the far ship turned, he said coldly, 'It is Henry Miller. He was at Trinity in my time and he killed Edward Taaffe in the Fifteen Acres when I was in my last year.'

'Miller? Yes, of course, my neighbour over by Caxley. He must be related to the Admiral – Miller is

MS III, 10

64

Lord Leyton's family name, and that person over there often spoke of a peerage going to some fairly close connexion. Cousin, of course: they would not be walking arm in arm, otherwise.' After a pause Jack went on, 'What do you mean by your Fifteen Acres?'

'It is a space in the Phoenix Park – you know the great park in Dublin, I am sure?' Jack nodded. 'And that is where people go, particularly the young men of Trinity, to settle matters of honour.'

'Just so: and he killed a gunner officer in Malta, too. He is said to be a very good shot; and he has capital pistols. I have heard him called Hair-Trigger Miller; and to be sure I have seen him bring down a great many pheasants.'

'Would you say he was a quarrelsome man, at all?'

'I scarcely know him. We are necessarily acquainted, but he is not the sort of man whose acquaintance I should value – in short, I do not like him. It is not the fighting. As you know, duels are much more usual in the army than with us, or even the Marines. And anyhow you and I have both been out from time to time . . . cannot top it the Holy Joe.' Jack stared out over the water and went on. 'For all I know he may be well enough liked in his regiment: but his reputation in the neighbourhood is so indifferent that I was astonished to learn that he had called on Edward and Christine when they settled in Medenham, and then at Woolcombe when Christine was staying there, with Edward so far in the north. I have no room to blackguard a man for incontinence, being no model myself: but there are limits . . . You know very well, Stephen, how much influence a man with a large household

MS III, 11

and a considerable estate can bring to bear on his dependents – his dependents' daughters – and there were some very ugly tales of girls in child being turned away. I *know* very little: yet his conduct does seem to match with the general reprobation.'

'He is not married, I take it?'

'No, nor ever has been. Being almost next in succession to the Leyton title, he is said to be saving himself up for some very brilliant match.'

'Can you square a man's valuing a peerage very highly with his going out and risking his life so often?'

'Yes, if he is an unusually resentful unloved creature and at the same time an uncommon good shot.'

'Sir, if you please,' said the officer of the watch, stepping aft and taking off his hat, 'Flag is breaking out a signal.' Speaking in the high, staccato, expressionless voice usual on such occasions, the duty midshipman piped up, 'Flag to *Suffolk*: Admiral invites Rear-Admiral and Doctor M-A-T-U-R-I-N to dinner at a quarter past three: repeat a quarter past three o'clock.'

'Rear-Admiral to flag: very happy,' said Jack in italics. Then he hurried aft to Stephen's point of discreet withdrawal. 'Stephen, I have engaged you to dine with the Admiral tomorrow: I hope you do not mind it?'

'I do not mind it, my dear: and it would make not odds if I did. We are all worms under the harrow, in *MS III, 12* the service: even you, Jack, scintillating in gold lace, are but one of us. *I say come, and he cometh: for I am a centurion.* I have met few admirals: some high, mighty and almost certainly constipated; others small, jolly, good company: reading men, even. Besides, I long for men's company: the prattle of the little girls –

much though I love them – drives me to an earlier and earlier breakfast, to a later and even later dinner, so that presently the two will meet, as they did in Avicenna's tale. They come to me with a pelagic crab, a starfish, a piece of common wrack, and standing by my side they cry, "Oh sir, pray tell us what it is," so that I am tempted to utter obscene blasphemy. Oh how I long for dear Jacob's return!'

'I believe our departure depends largely on that,' said Jack gravely; and then after a pause, 'I tell you what, Stephen,' he cried, 'it is long since we had a real great-gun exercise. The last powder-hoy, for a trifle of whiskey – you know the Irish drink, Stephen, I am sure?'

'I have never heard of it,' said Stephen.

'– gave us a little surplus, so that the gunner is actually at a loss to stow it: nothing could be happier. And if that does not deafen, astound and silence the little girls there is the Devil in it. I shall give orders directly. The whole *shooting-match*!" Jack did not often stumble on a witticism, and this one gave him particular delight: he repeated it twice.

The whole shooting-match it was, indeed: *Suffolk* might not have been called a very taut ship, nor more than ordinarily crack, but she could never have been likened to the Margate hoy; and in any case she now carried many Surprises, long used to their captain's ways and his rigid insistence upon very high standards indeed. The breeze being both steady and favourable Jack laid on his favourite, most profitable form of exercise, one calculated to promote zeal, speed and above all accuracy, to knit a gun-crew into

MS III, 13

an immensely cooperative whole – never a word passing, never a word called for – and to promote the most valuable sort of competition. The most experienced gun-captains and the older, wiser midshipmen were at the three forward guns; and bitter shame would fall upon any following gun that could not keep up with them in speed or accuracy.

The first three guns had been ordered to fire high, to leave something for the rest of the broadside; and Jack, as a particular treat, silencer or gob-stopper for the little girls, had with Mr Meares the gunner contrived a flimsy but coherent structure that under very light and worn-out canvas would drift until it was abreast of the man-of-war, which would then pound it with the most rapid broadside compatible with the *Suffolk*'s timbers – a broadside rolling, but only just rolling.

'Target's away,' hailed the foretopmast lookout. 'On deck, there, target's away.'

'From forward aft as she bears,' called Jack; and there was a long, tense silence, broken only by the gentle wind in the rigging. The little girls, in white frocks, stood on tip-toe: just behind them Sophie and Christine, almost equally tense. The captain of Number One glared along his sights, the lanyard in his right hand, his left making very slight delicate motions to swivel or elevate the huge gun-barrel right or left, up or down a trifle. 'Fire!' he cried and heaved on the lanyard: the hammer shot forward and with barely a perceptible pause the gun uttered its prodigious roar, a great jet of smoke and flame enveloping the cannon-ball and the gun-carriage and cannon raced inboard with a screech of trunions under the arched bodies of the crew until

the whole was brought up short with a great twang of
the tackles; but already there were immensely active
hands cleaning any smouldering remnants from the
gun, swabbing the barrel, ramming down the next
charge of powder, then the ball, then the wads, well
thumped down, the crew barely pausing for breath but
running the whole mass up against the side with a
crash, where the gun-captain pricked and primed his
cock, unmoved by the truly appalling discharge of his
right-hand neighbour as he and his mates made all fast
and levelled the warm gun again.

The firing went clean down the battleship's side at a
fine even pace, and even the aftermost piece had its
shot at the frail remnant that drifted by. But by then
the little girls had almost no voice to screech with nor
even the emotional power to do so: the enormous and
repeated din, the vibration of the ship and the air, the
great flashes and the dense clouds of smoke drifting
away to leeward had overpowered them; and the near-
stupefaction of their elders was very impressive too.
Sophie had seen sloops and moderate frigates at gun-
exercise, but never a ship of the line, and she was quite
remarkably perturbed, not only by the unconscionable
din but infinitely more by the reflection that this was
what his profession inflicted upon her husband: or at
least the way of life to which it exposed him. Christine,
to to be sure, had fired many and many a fowling-piece
and even upon occasion a rifled gun, but nothing
imaginably on this scale, and she remained quite
mute, holding Brigid's hand, until after a good deal of
calling-out right forward the cry came down, 'On
deck, on deck there. Target's away, sir.'

So it was, a great long affair of all kinds of old casks and nameless objects from the entire squadron clapped together and furnished with enough cloth of a sort to carry the whole downwind. The target appeared on the starboard bow, towed by boats that cast off as soon as it was well on course. An active intelligent master's mate ran down the broadside: 'No fire until the Admiral gives the word: then count MS III, 15 * two between each shot.'

MS III, 15a A profound silence: the target drifted half way down the *Suffolk*'s length. 'Fire,' said Jack.

The first gun and before it quite ran in the second and so clear along down to the last: and when the smoke cleared and the last repeated echo died away there was nothing but tossing water to be seen. The little girls had strength enough to utter a last gasping 'Oh,' and then they were led away, exhausted: but not before a furious Killick had appeared on the quarterdeck waving a full-dress coat. 'Which I had it all laid out a quarter of an hour long past. Ain't you got . . .' He was going to say 'no shame?' but disapproving looks, coupled with Jack's compliance and a call for the barge checked his zeal.

With a following breeze and a very well-inclined crew the barge fairly skimmed across the sea, hooking on only a matter of seconds late. In any case Lord Leyton was in a good mood – he could be jovial and

* The manuscript here has been considerably reworked by the author. Pages *MS III, 15* and *MS III, 15a* (both marked by O'Brian as page 15 of Chapter Three) are different versions of the same material. *MS III, 15* seems to be the later draft, as it corresponds more closely to the typsescript.

he could be damned crabbed: but this was a good day. He had heard much of Dr Maturin's acquaintance, close acquaintance, with Prince William, who, in view of his elder brother's constitution, was likely to be king in the early forseeable future. 'Well, Aubrey,' he cried giving his guest a hand as he came aboard, 'you very nearly split the heavens with that damned great rolling broadside – God's my life, thunder and lightning was nothing to compare. Don't I wish you may not have started more than a dozen of your timbers, ha, ha, ha! And don't I wish you may have come by your powder honestly, ha, ha, ha, ha! Allow me to present my young cousin Randolph Miller' – beckoning to a soldier in regimentals, smiling just behind him. 'But of course you know him already, you are neighbours in the country.'

'How do you do, sir?' said Jack, accepting Miller's proffered hand.

MS III, 16

'And this, sir, is Dr Maturin, I presume?' said Lord Leyton. 'How kind of you to come. I have had a particular desire to meet you ever since the Duke of Clarence told me you were a most uncommonly learned man. I am not particularly learned myself, but I love to surround myself with those that are. May I introduce you to Captain Miller, my cousin Randolph – but now I come to reflect, perhaps a Doctor of Medicine takes rank over a simple soldier . . .'

'Not at all, my lord: but it so happens that we were at Trinity at much the same time, so I already have that honour.'

'Indeed he was: Trinity College, Dublin. Well then, if he too were at Trinity, then he too is one of the learned

71

– it stands to reason. And I dare say he can split an infinitive as quick as any man. But may I introduce . . .'

Presently they were called to the Admiral's truly splendid dining-cabin, which could seat ten people easily, each with a servant behind his chair and plenty of room for those who came hurrying in with dishes and tureens, sauceboats, trays of bread and of course very large quantities of wine – a grateful Sancerre with the bonito, an Haut-Brion with the admirable duck and an ancient burgundy with the roast beef: unhappily it was corked. The chaplain on Stephen's right murmured something about 'a quaint reminiscence of antiquity' and Jack did not empty his glass; but their host took no notice of his formal first sip and none of his officers showed any sign of awareness. 'Stoicism?' asked Stephen privately. 'Dislike of offending the great man? Discipline? Stark insensibility?'

When it came to the port, however, the case was altered: all hands, including the parson, drank eagerly; and when they reached the loyal toast there was no man who did not drain his brimming glass and murmur, 'God bless him,' with real feeling, and emptied it.

MS III, 17

After this ceremony and the chaplain's grace, Lord Leyton observed that although the glass was sinking it was still quite a fine afternoon, and some of them might like to take their coffee, and perhaps some brandy, on deck.

There were general sounds of agreement, a general movement, though with due regard for precedence, and the Admiral keeping Jack by his side until the room was free, said, in answer to his thanks and congratulations, 'Not at all, not at all, my dear fellow

– a very simple little feast: though I must admit that they have capital beef in these part. But did you notice anything about the burgundy?'

'No, sir: capital wine.'

'Well, I am glad of that. For a moment I thought – but, however, what I wanted to tell you before coffee was that I should like you to weigh on the ebb and to proceed to Saint Helena under a very easy sail and there to wait in that damned uneasy roadstead until you see me plain. Then you must weigh and carry on for the Cape: there is not room for all three squadrons to lie there safely together in a strong sou'wester. But that will already make a very impressive show of force, I believe.'

'Certainly, sir.'

'And then I should like you to take my nephew along with you. As you may know, he has been given an appointment at the Cape, and the sooner he is there the better – you might even lend him your tender for the last few days, if the wind drops, as it so often does as you approach the coast. Now let us hurry on deck, before all those God-damned soldiers have drunk all the brandy.'

On deck Captain Miller at once came up to Jack and said, 'Sir, I hear with great pleasure that Mrs Aubrey and Mrs Wood are both aboard you, and that *MS III, 17a** perhaps we may be shipmates far as the Cape. Allow me to fetch you a glass of brandy.' Coming back with the glass in his hand he cried, 'My dear cousin has just

* The first paragraph of *MS III, 17a* here was eliminated in the author's typescript version.

told me that you will be so very kind as to take me with you. Thank you very much indeed. I did myself the pleasure of waiting on Mr Heatherleigh when he and his sister – whom I already knew and admired from my days in Sierra Leone – were settling at Medenham; and later I called on Mrs Aubrey and Mrs Wood at Woolcombe when you were still at sea – I must congratulate you on your children, sir.'

Jack looked at him with some surprise. Their degree of acquaintance did not warrant anything like this familiarity. 'Has the man drunk too much?' he wondered inwardly: aloud he said, 'Forgive me, if you please,' and walked across the deck to where Dr Maturin was listening sullenly to Lord Leyton's harangue – his detailed explanation of how he was going to tell Napoleon how he could have avoided defeat at Waterloo. 'Aubrey,' cried Leyton, turning, 'cannot you persuade or even order Dr Maturin to stay while I have my interview with the Emperor – with General Buonaparte, I should say? I can read the French pretty well, with a dictionary at hand, but I cannot speak it with anything like the Doctor's fluency.'

'Oh come, my lord,' said Stephen, 'what you say sounds

MS III, 18

[*The typescript ends here. The chapter continues without conclusion on MSS III, 18–26.*]

FACSIMILE OF THE MANUSCRIPT

Chapter One

Chapter I

Stephen Maturin screwed up to his writing desk once again: he had been called away to attend to one of the ship's boys, who had contrived to skin himself in the foretop by taking the maul from its place, tossing it to a considerable height and so misjudging the revolutions as it fell that the massive head struck him down, speechless and unnaturally pale. Stephen dressed the wound, such as it was (more bruise than blood and no bone broken) and said to his loblolly boy 'Poll, tell Dr Jacob when he comes back, that this boy is to have no grog for the next three days and tomorrow he may keep his hammock.' Dr Jacob, the surgeon's mate, was away visiting friends aboard the frigate's tender, that rapid and windwardly Chesapeake schooner Ringle, and Stephen glanced in her direction from the starboard bow, before going down from the brilliance of noon to the comparatively sombre cabin which he shared with Jack Aubrey.

He had already written My dear Christine before he was called away, and he had dated the letter Surprise, at sea, in Magellan's Strait. At his first sitting down he had meant to tell her, with what skill he could command, of the extraordinary beauty of the weather, and of the strait, ordinarily so forbidding: he should certainly have spoken of the favourable wind that had allowed them to keep topgallantsails abroad ever since the morning watch; but above all he should have dwelt upon the happiness that filled the ship, homeward bound after a long, arduous and most uncommonly dangerous voyage, a well-found ship commanded by a right seaman, a well-liked, deeply respected fighting Captain who, moreover, was soon to hoist his flag. There was no secret about this: Captain Aubrey's first unrestrained cries of delight had not escaped his steward or anyone else within a range of twenty yards; nor had the *if unwonted* floods of rum, the feasts in cabin, gunroom and midshipmen's

on receipt of the blessed signal / message

7. fo'c'sle

berth; and the saved blue flag itself lay openly on the forecastle, shaded from too fierce a sun, from untimely drops of spray, by an awning, the sailmaker and his mates, the ship's tailor and his, activating it with minute stitches, While every hand aboard added half an inch of the seam around its ample verge. It was considered the handsomest ensign in the service

at least

But for the moment the flag was was absent from Stephen's mind: indeed the mind itself was in a singular state of absence, hesitation, even stupidity. Before being called to that wretched boy he had known the general trend of the points that were to follow the words that lay there before them, but now he was filled with doubt and to give his wits to time to settle and clarify he mended his pen, clipping its end with a minute pair of metal jaws made for the purpose and trimming the sides with a lancet capable of splitting a hair.

Yet the right free, easy, candid expressions would not come, though the Christine in question was very dear to him: Stephen had long practised medicine, a calling in which discretion is often of great importance; but for an even longer time, if time is to be measured by slites, he had been an intelligence agent, and here discretion was of the very essence, since an unguarded/slip might lead to the agent's death and the death, the other hideous death, of his friends and the destruction of their cause.

word or

He sat down, his expression still tolerably blank: he wore lean, middle-sized man, unremarkable, of mixed Catalan and Irish origin, but it was the tropical sun and the sea air that accounted for his dark complexion not any mixture of Moorish blood, for although his birth was illegitimate (which weighed upon him) his ancestors had been Christians time out of mind. A man of something less than forty, though he looked older as his mind wrestled with the difficulties of giving the intelligent woman he longed to marry a coherent, plausible account of the Surprise's activities and of her present return, mission accomplished: for when Captain Aubrey joined the South African squadron in the River Plate, going aboard HMS Suffolk, taking command of her, and hoisting or causing to be hoisted his flag hoisted at the mizzen, that would turn him into that glorious creature a rear-admiral

?

a receipt
a certificate from the beam complaint game and power

the likelihood, the virtual certainty, was that HM *Surprise* should go return home, carrying Jack Aubrey's official dispatch, letters home from those who could write, two young men who were to pass for lieutenants. and a great number of papers that justified the expenditure or replacement of the every item in ship's unbelievably complex expensive gear: furnishings and supplies from pistol flints to great roundshot a innumerable blocks. There was also a flat, factual account day by day account of the *Surprise's* meetings with the Chilean authorities and of her proceedings.

She had arrived in Chile after a long and arduous voyage round the Horn. She was one of the smaller frigates, carrying no more than 28 great guns, and although in the right hands she was a most outstanding sailer she had been sold out of the service when the heavier craft were built and Stephen had bought her, so there she was, eminently seaworthy and available for hire to the Hydrographical Service of the Admiralty once Napoleon had been dealt with and the western world was at something like peace

Her ostensible function was to survey and chart the little known coasts and innumerable islands of the recently independent republic of Chile and to help form its navy, training the young officers All this was perfectly avowable and even praiseworthy. But the voyage had other aspects that were never distinctly laid down in written orders but that were implied and understood on both sides — and her total candour was wholly out of the question, so that Stephen's letter home could obviously not be all he wished

In the first place, through Stephen's innumerable connexions Jack had been appointed commander in chief of the Chilean navy as well as Admiralty hydrographer, but the frigate's voyage to had been slow and when she reached Chile she found that the situation had changed remarkably. Apart from anything else she met with a bewildering number of juntas, of more or less independent governing bodies belonging to wholly different political parties, one of which had appointed its own commander in chief though all were

to England

meadow
unadorned

alarmed, surprised, displeased

would then return home

HORED

that Surprise, a former Royal Naval frigate, sold out of the service, bought by Maturin himself, and for this ocean sailing as a surveying hydrographical vessel with the purpose of laying down the ill-charted coasts and islands of the recently independent republics of Chile and of helping to form a new Chilean navy, training the young officers. The Surprise was met with a bewildering number of more or less governing bodies of widely-differing political parties, and with the ever-present threat of Peruvian invasion by land or sea or both – Peru at that time still being ruled from Lima by the Spanish king's viceroy, and still possessed a powerful, fully trained navy.

After a very great number of vicissitudes, changes of government and so on it appeared to Jack Aubrey – who had had many a mean and hard but precious hills in the way of formal exact written instructions – that the best way of preserving the Chilean republic and above all of protecting his beloved infant Chilean navy was to attack the Peruvians in their port of Callao and if possible to cut out their big frigate, an Esmeralda, the best armed man-of-war on the Pacific coast of America. – This he did with extraordinary success. though at the risk of his life. bringing the big Esmeralda back to Valparaiso. But although he was very much flattered and caressed, he was treated very shabbily: his men were not paid: they were denied their prize-money from various sources: and upon some pretext his ship was threatened with impoundment. But though Jack was sometimes behaved like a simpleton by land, and though he was often swindled ashore, he was sea-wise, and having provisioned and stored his ship with enough to carry her home, he issued an ultimatum to the Chileans: either his men must have their due by a given date or he should sail away. They were not paid, and he did sail away. Yet although the Surprise's voyage had the appearance of a failure, in fact the Spanish hold in South America was broken: and although there had not been the Admiralty's direct order, the result gave great pleasure in the right quarters.

①

obscured by the fear of a Peruvian invasion by land or sea or both; Peru
was still ruled by the Spanish King's viceroy in Lima, and it still possessed
a powerful, well-trained navy.

After a very great number of vicissitudes, changes of ministry,
and so on it appeared to Jack that since his main duty, often expressed
in London but never committed to writing, was to preserve the *independent* Chilean
republic, the best way of doing so and at the same time of protecting
his beloved infant Chilean navy was to attack the Peruvians in their
port of Callao and if possible to cut out their big frigate *Esmeralda*,
far heaviest, best-armed man-of-war on the Pacific coast of America.
This he did with extraordinary success, at the risk of his life; and he
brought the *Esmeralda* back to Valparaiso. He was much flattered and
caressed; but he was treated very shabbily indeed: his men were not
paid, they were denied their prize-money from various sources; and upon
some pretext his ship was threatened with impoundment *Yet though*
Jack sometimes behaved like a simpleton by land, and though he
was often swindled ashore, he was sea-wise, and having provisioned
and stored his ship with ~~everything needed to carry her~~ the barest supplies at least to
handed the Chileans an ultimatum: either his men must have their
due by a given date or he should sail away. They were not
paid, and he did sail away *Yet although* the *Surprise's*
voyage had something of the appearance of a failure, in fact the
Spanish hold on South America was broken: and although there
had not been the Admiralty's direct orders, the result gave immense
satisfaction pleasure in the ~~right~~ proper quarters.

Furthermore Jack had aboard a singularly amiable young man, *and gifted*
the unacknowledged but much beloved illegitimate son of Prince
William, Admiral the Duke of Clarence, a zealous sailor and almost
certain to be King after his brother's death. Clarence had a
great respect for Captain Aubrey (some of Jack's actions were indeed

extraordinarily brilliant), and though Dr Maturin, who had treated His Highness for a variety of diseases, mostly discreditable, had begged Jack to take the boy on this voyage: and young Blanco had distinguished himself as much as any loving naval father could have wished, cutting the Esmeralda's cable and carrying her out under fire.

Yet even this was not all: on the Pacific coast Jack and Stephen had met with a small stout vessel filled with fellow members of the Royal Society, two of whom, ornithologists, were determined to cross the narrow isthmus of Panama and return to London by the Atlantic. And these excellent creatures had agreed to take Jack's dispatches — the news of his famous victory and the preservation of Chile — back to the Admiralty, then in the process of forming a South African squadron. Maturin and his chief, the head of Naval Intelligence, had long since established a system of rapid communication across the Andes, and it was thanks to this arrangement that Jack had received the *beautiful* signal requiring him 'to proceed to the River Plate, there to go aboard HMS Suffolk, taking command of her and hoisting his flag, blue at the mizzen' that had spread such happiness throughout the ship

Chilean

Yet though the ephemeral ministry had fallen, to be replaced by some one of their many rivals, the satisfaction had by no means general: there were many who regretted their red frocks and their declared policies. Furthermore this feeling was not confined to Chile: there were many Chilean refugees and many of their Argentinian friends who had resented the Englishmen's presence and who now even more bitterly resented their absence — Argentinian to say nothing of those many many Argentinians who so plainly remembered the British capture of Buenos Aires and the even greater number of those who looked upon them as vile heretics, given to cursing the Holy Father almost every day.

Both Maturin and Jacob had caught wind of this feeling — *chiefly* during their very beautiful passage of the Straits and the *evening* afternoon before they were to put in to San Pedro. a small sealing and fishing port anchorage at the bottom of an inlet on the northern shore with some sheltered arable land behind it famous for potatoes and cabbages on the one hand and prodigious messels and crayfish on the other. Stephen said 'My dear Jack, in the backwoods of America they say that an evil reputation is like an inextinguishable sept; and we have been so maligned on the Pacific coast that you might think it prudent to arm the boats, or even to hale the ship so close to the strand that your great guns command the whole entire settlement.'

In the event the few inhabitants of San Pedro did not choose to take challenge a powerful man of war. moored broadside on before their settlement. nor the cutlass-bear powerful, cutlass-bearing seamen who walked about along the cuay. But although most of them were at least partially Tierra del Fuegian and although none of them could have had any first-hand knowledge of recent events they were sullen and unfriendly, yielding only a few indifferent potatoes and wilted cabbages at an exor exorbitant pot price. However the ship did top up her water from clear, free-running stream, and still with this blessed westerly breeze she pursued her long, wearisome course through the strait. Jack, Hanson and Daniels perpetually taking bearings, soundings, views of the shore (icy to the southward, often raining to the north) and establishing a truly remarkable chart.

Stephen, who had no abilities whatsoever in this direction, confined himself to his medical duties of course (slight they were, with a healthy crew and such an able assistant as Jacob), to watching and sometimes dissecting the birds, mammals, and marine plants and creatures on the shore of the strait, and much of these he added to his letter to Christine, she being the only woman of his acquaintance who knew the difference between a jackass penguin and a macaroni and who thoroughly delighted in the knowledge,

here I must have a reasonably comprehensive account of the strait's natural history. It to be gathered from [Jotuffi?] book, Darwin, & than Brit

the parrots can appear in number (+ other sexotica ? humming birds) in a skreecing wind from a NW (or wherever)

It could extend to 200 words   ? eaten

He was reasonably well engaged with this letter one afternoon after dinner when Jack, abandoning his fiddle, returned to his surgery, and Stephen, closing his passage on Port Egmont hens, lifted his head to Hanson's reiterated 'Sir, if you please.'

'Why, Mister Rea?' — for Horatio Hanson was acting master of & oby — 'I fear you have been waiting. I never heard you.'

'Not at all, sir: it was only that Dr Jacob feared you might have overlooked your appointment.' At this moment a ting chime could be heard in each watch, for both possessed of wonderfully accurate repeating watches, the one given to Stephen by his grandfather, the other to Hanson by Prince William. 'God love us all and may I be forgiven.' cried Stephen leaping up. 'It is half eleven - I am so late.'

'Mind your cap, sir.' said Hanson, steadying him. 'It is blowing up uncommon stiff from the near WNW - has veered like fools in half an hour, and Ringle is reefing hard.'

They made their way forward to the fairly well-lit & and now vacant space in the sickberth which the surgeons reserved for anatomizing — they were busy on a singular, probably undescribed small dolphin and as they carefully pared away, separated and described the muscular parts so they gave them to the cook's mates, standing there with buckets. The bones they kept for themselves. But presently they were obliged to stop. The ship's motion was too great; and in spite of all their skill and care, the deck was awash — their cutting by no means accurate.

'We are making ready to lie to, sir.' said Hanson in his ear. 'And the Captain says he will pass the word when it is fit for you to come on deck. In the mean time he desires you would shelter and so Jacob and stand by to deal with casualties.'

The first, to his infinite shame, was Harding, the first lieutenant — a straightforward broken fibula and tibia, which they very soon splinted and

Febru o

①

bound up. then came the usual series of bumps and bruises, diminishing
as the furious gust blew itself out and ending with the Captain's compliments
brought by Awkward Davies, and if now he chose to come on deck he
would a 'sight like a madhouse's washing-day - God love us - what
rigging we have fast eluded, stuffed, with furious parrots and God knows
what, in which I am to bring you and cap 300 lashes if you fall.'

Long, long had Stephen heard of the little parrots of S South America
forest. but he had never seen one and nor he would fairly have leapt on
deck but for Davies' powerful restraining hand

more. perhaps 200 more, when more I know

For two and even three days after that furious blast the waters of
the Strait remained strong, turbulent, particularly in the narrows, and
great beds of kelp, apparently torn loose floated on every hand, sometimes
endangering the rudder, sometimes checking their [wing]/and always
distinctive birds, cetaceans, and ordinary level-headed fishes
Nevertheless their whole passage before they turned north, well out in the
full Atlantic, took them only three hours more than nine days.

'We are making pretty good time.' said Jack. 'and I think we
may look into Port Desire and Bahia Blanca without keep the Admiral
waiting. He was not to sail till the twelfth.'

'Would you ever tell me, has he a numerous fleet?'

'Pretty considerable: three squadrons, of which ours, to sure, is
of course the smallest - but, Stephen, do not think for a moment that
I complain. Of course it is the smallest. Every blue. But even it bore
half the size I should have given my right hand for it. Good Lord above:
a flag at last! It was amazingly kind of them. Do not think for a
moment that I complain, dear Stephen.'

'It had not occurred to me at all, at all.' said Stephen. And

9

he went on. 'Since my ill-bred questions is so prosperous - and to be sure it is very ill-bred indeed - may I ask why you mean to stop at the South American ports if, when I understood you to say we could sail home with what was in the hold?'

'Why, for fresh water and fresh meat, of course: to say nothing of vegetables and fruit. We could ~~prefer~~ probably have got home, of course, but rachitious, half-starved and rotten with scurvy: but that was a desperate stroke ~~for~~ in a ~~God~~-damned desperate situation, one that a man could not stand. But now the case is altered. I am to join Lord Leyton in the River Plate, and I make no doubt - for he is a very active officer, as I know full well - that he will take us down and to that across to the Cape with the utmost despatch, and I prefer to be ready to weigh at the first hail of a signal, with the last case of bread biscuit aboard and a well-fed active crew — no short beer will be allowed.'

healthy

'But, my dear, Surprise is to go home, as you very well know, with your despatches and all our letters however; and once there she reverts to the station of a British ship. Ever since we left off Magellan's Strait ~~the people~~ and steered north the people have become increasingly aware of this, and the happiness that filled the frigate has sensibly diminished day by day. You & I know how unhappy our men from Shelmerston were when they were paid off into the peace, and how wonderfully they revived when you took them aboard.'

'Certainly I know it very well, and I am going to use all what interest I may have to have her back in the service. The squadron is pitifully short of frigates, and since I understand that our duty elsewhere there is the protection of the Russian and ~~the~~ Chinese ~~trade~~, nothing could be more useful than a nimble weatherly ship like Surprise. And I beg you will do the same. But even if we cannot succeed directly, I am allowed my bargemen and a good many others — I have little doubt that I shall loose a score or so of the rest among my friends. And for those that are left, if any are left, merchant shipping has revived wonderfully, and a seaman with a good character from the Royal Navy will not want long for a berth.'

Just as it had been Hanson who first sighted Cape Pilar on their eastward leg, at the very opening of the strait, so it was his particular friend Daniel who, splashing his water below in the fore/topgallant crosstrees, caught the leading-marks for Port Desire in his glass, checked it twice and called

①

'On deck there. On deck: St Paul's rock bears to fathom under on the larboard bow. Dim. Comes & goes.'

It came and went because of a heavy sea inshore that covered in enlarged form time to time. Y not with green water then with foam; and although it necessitated somewhat inshore, the frigate had an uneasy time of it, mooring in the sullen turbulence this side of the primitive mole — surly waters from some untimely flash-flood.

'I once saw a rhea here, some way inland,' observed Stephen, as he and Jacob were walking along the main street (obscurely strewn with drowned dogs) to speak to the port-captain about water and vegetables. 'Indeed?'

a S. American ostrich, somewhat unlike the African ... , now unknown ... 'Ah?' ... ... 'I believe them in the captain's here

He half rose when they came in, but he was far from cordial and he said that he would not recommend the town water after this upset deodoré flood and all the nastiness it brought.

Stephen spoke about the country inland, a hacienda he had visited, the kindness of the people. He and the others were of course speaking Spanish and after a while the port-captain said that there happened to be a clean spring at no great distance, but they would have to pay the proprietor a fee. 'It is not for myself, you understand — I am astonishingly generous, generous to a S/c fault, even lavish...' He spoke of his faults at some length and then, having called for coffee, he asked in a more confidential, almost affectionate tone, 'Do they, obviously old and trained Christians, consort, consort with these vile heretics?' And when Stephen made the usual gestures of extreme poverty, rubbing the thumb over knuckle, the captain shook his head, saying 'Ah, when the Devil drives... I shall send my boy with the men to Anneta's spring, but they must be very respectful to her and pluck off their hats. Her sister Helene, who is a werewolf, will provide the cabbages.'

So she did, from upstanding plants, but without the least appearance of pleasure or (perhaps understandably) of common humanity, and both in their transaction and in a far olive along the edge of the market noticed a sullenness, a sleepy inclination to stare, muttering; while after some of these transactions the sellers could be seen to wash the coins or rub them industriously on the greasy planks, gritty ... foot.

Even *the Surprise*, with her singularly faint lines and her 36-gun frigate's towering mainmast had not been so recognizable to a sailor's eye. Her ensign would have identified her almost anywhere in the world, for on reverting to her function as a survey-vessel under Admiralty command she had also reverted to the white ensign. At Bahia Blanca, their next port of call, Stephen, who was the natural emissary on such occasions, reported the same sullen antipathy, not unmingled with a reluctance to sell, exorbitant prices, and injurious expressions.

'Brother, you are playing at least a half-tone too high,' said Jack that evening as they sailed away after an early supper.

'Am I?' cried Stephen, looking attentively at his fingers & lowering the slow. 'So I am. I do beg your pardon. It is the sheer bitterness of my soul that makes it wail, I fear.'

'I am so sorry to impose these ~~daily~~ odious duties upon you, Stephen — pray take a sup of port — but you know, of course you know only too well, that when you and all your people have been without long enough you will descend to the basest means to relieve them.'

'I am not sure that ~~that is~~ ^the expression^ altogether civil: but be that as it may, I will tell you, Jack, that if they are bad in Port Desire and worse in Bahia, they are likely to be downright outrageous in the River Plate. For, ^when you^ ^enter^ I understand you aright, we are to join — meet the South African ^ships^ ~~squadron~~, right up against the city. Yet if I am not mistaken we are likely to be there well before Lord Leyton — well before even your little squadron . . .'

'What the Devil do you mean my little ~~squadron~~? It is a perfectly normal squadron, if rather large, than otherwise. Two ships of the line apart from Suffolk, a fifty-gun ship, are considerable ships of war . . .'

'Hush, hush, Jack. Never fly into a passion, soul,' said Stephen, seeing that his friend was quite seriously annoyed. 'Sure, you must know after all this time that we use little as an endearment — a meliorative term, as one says my little purse to a handsome Amazon that weighs fifteen stone in her ship. So we arrive. do you follow me, now?, well before her lordship, whom God preserve, and our natural allies, all because of our commendable zeal. Now let me beg you, for all love, to moor your ship close in against the southern shore, and refrain to cover us as it were among the shallows there, and never to slid ashore for so much as an egg, an egg: for in a considerable city fanaticism and resentment can swell to a most surprising and horrible extent.

At the end of his particularly grave allegro, Jack put down his bow and said 'Should you dislike it very much if we were to leave Bahia out of our plans? Our water, and the cabbages have held out uncommon well and I had as soon push on Quick Rhuck, if you understand me, to the River Plate, where there are all sorts - it a great resort of merchantmen and all sorts of people that supply their wants, chandlers and the like: you are not dependent on the local werewolf. Not that I have anything to say against werewolves: the gentlewoman were perfectly civil, and her cabbage have stood up admirably.'

'I should not mind it at all. Bahia has, by all accounts some tolerable sloanes, but nothing in the way of lakes or marshland with stinking miliano: I had Jacob & I have an immense amount of sorting, classifying, and preserving to do, and I had as soon sail on northward - quickly, as you put it so well, to quickly pulling our collection in order.

Gently indeed they sailed along, with gentle breezes that wafted them & generally northward to ever warmer seas. Little activity was called for, apart from the nice adjustment of the sails, and although the exact routine of the ship was never relaxed nor her strict rules of cleanliness, these long sunny days with a soldier's wind seemed to many the ideal of a seaman's life. — regular, steady, traditional meals with the exact allowance of grog; hornpipes in the last dog-watch, the deep melody of the Captain's cello from the cabin and the cheerful sound of the gunroom's dinner. the future lost in the haze somewhere north of the equator.

So these golden days went by, and Stephen's mound of tiny skins mounted up, very carefully dried and treated against insects, the voracious

6

1

cockroaches that lurked in the ultimate recesses of the hold, their
survivors breeding with extraordinary rapidity

By the time they were in flying-fish water again, the *Surprise*
and her people had settled down to this very agreeable form of
life — some few cases of sunburn (or moon-pull by night) to
occupy Poll Skeeping and Maggie, and a series of small deep
painful wounds or rather hook-billed bites from those parakeets that
did not choose to be tamed, but for once, for once no steady
dosing for the pox. With a perfectly competent, conscientious
by no means tyrannical first lieutenant Jack Aubrey and his
clerk could devote their hours to gathering all the scattered surveying
material from its notebooks and journal and cast it in the regular
form most valued by the Hydrographical Department. They were
quite near the end of their immense immense extent, at the northern
tip of the Chonos Archipelago, surveyed with a team of zealous
and remarkably amiable young Chilean officer-cadets when the
expected news came below. With the master's duty, Mr Wells
begged to tell the Captain Aubrey that the leading marks for the
River Plate were clear from the masthead

They were clearer still by the last dog-watch, when the declining
sun lit them from behind; and in the morning they were well
upon into the white vast bay. All day, with a favouring breeze,
they sailed up it until both shores could be seen and a fair
amount of shipping: but never a sign of a man-of-war.

Farther, farther, with no more than topsails now: a pause
for dinner; and drinking coffee on deck afterwards Jack said to
Stephen 'May I ask you and Dr Jacob to run up to the island
with Wantage and make sure that our salute will be returned? This
is so curious a reception that I should like to make certain.'
Mr Harding, please to be so good as to leave lower the blue cutter over
the side.'

But while the coxswain & was summoning the cutter's crew Harding
yet

said to Jack. 'Forgive me, sir, but I believe I see a craft of cleanly form
the lee side. Yes, sir.' lowering his glass. 'I think it is one of
their medicoes and a couple of dirty mates. He peered again 'Yes,
a dirty, ill-looking & crew in a dirty ill-looking craft.'

They did not improve on closer acquaintance: at fifty yards from
the frigate's side a mean sloop up and bawled 'Quarantine.'

Hardly had a ladder put over and the leading man, in a black
coat and a yellow wig, followed by a youth with an ink-horn,
came aboard quite nimbly. 'Dr Quental,' he said, very loud,
'Health. Speak Portuguese?' Wanting, who was fluent in a language,
made as if to answer but Stephen checked her. 'I am the surgeon
of this ship,' he said. 'Dr Maturin, at your service. I do not
have the pleasure of speaking Portuguese but I should be happy to
converse answer any question you choose to ask, in Latin; so much
so that

Dr Quental put a reasonably good face on he could and if not with
more ease than the company expected he & repeated a list of various
classes of diseases — exanthematici, critici, phlogistici, dolorosi
mentales, quietales motorii, suppres suppressorii, evacuatorii
deformes, vitia. Stephen gently all of what Stephen gravely
considered, shaking his head in each instance and desired them to
& Quental to come below and view what invalids the ship possessed.
Poll Skeepus and Maggie had had plenty of time = there few patient
(all with strains, broken bones & one gross toothache, to be dealt with
tomorrow, when the armourer should have forged fashioned suitably
(his particular point)
massive forceps) were suitably cleaned brushed or rigid in their cots
washed, brushed and incog and incog'd of movement, almost of drawing
breath. Dr Quental was suitably impressed, suitably gratified
by a draught of rum, so happy to accept the gift of a neat, cased
French amputating saw, and perfectly willing to give Stephen a clean
                                              wrote
bill of health. On having to also gave it in his considered
opinion that the fort would not hesitate to answer the ship's
salute; and, having sealed the Latin with some ease, he
told Stephen that he was an anti-cleric, that he had nothing to say

for example . or blacks, or even   ① 15

to religious intolerance and that he jeered away that there were very good
men everywhere . even among Jews / or worse .

the MS p 17 follows the typed MS as follows:

is slipped p 15 & 16

from this point I continued
with the typewriter : I have
change back to this again

pp 15 & 16 not
in TS

my typing went on to the bottom of p 16 and now I think I must return to p

space

In the close-packed communities that made up the crew of a man-of-war there was extremely little privacy: they ate, slept, washed, relieved themselves in public; in public they were flogged unless they happened to be officers, and a severe admonition was very soon known throughout the ship. Each man or boy knew exactly what the others earned and how much the married men sent home. And although the officers sometimes had private means, and were sometimes unwilling to speak of them, they also had servants, who knew whether their masters were bearing hard up, bearing hard up for Poverty Bay or spreading all canvas for Port Lavish itself. The paternity order which had brought many hands about ...

a subject well repeated not

There were few surprises therefore who were much astonished at the very strong similarity between the Nuncio and his host. It was perfectly well known that the younger man was one of Mr Stephens Aubrey's indiscretion when, as a long-legged youth, he had served on the South African station, and that the boy, brought up by Catholic missionaries in Mozambique, had presented himself to his father in the West Indies, bearing the present of a heathen charm (a ju-ju) that had kept jack alive through some really desperate encounters. Killick was of course a fount and a reasonably honest fount of information. Much of it derived from Barret Bonden. Jackie coxswain and without these out of mind, a ... source of much greater value.

from his affectionate mother

From this general history, therefore, what newcomer there was in that long harbour-watch. It learnt that the good fathers having taught Sam his letters — the language he picked up with no sort of trouble — and a considerable amount of Latin, declined him for the minor orders but — for nothing more. because of his illegitimate birth: but Stephen Maturin who thought a bastard himself was very well connected indeed and he obtained a dispensation for the young man, to whom he was much attached and Sam had risen with extraordinary speed. To be sure, he was very intelligent and very good-natured; but he was also very black, shining black; and this was a time when a strong current of opinion in the Church felt that the influence of a rapidly increasing black world should receive marked notice. On the merely practical side, the very, very large number of black

from the sun

man and women, slaves or hired labourers, particularly in
South America, an act necessary influence the Balance of power
in them. Father Pauw, who was a natural-born linguist,
had already done excellent work in Brazil; and so now he
was sent to the Argentine with greetings, and perhaps some good
advice to those who were, or who were about to be, in power.

Chapter Two

XXI

Chapter II

⑪

'By God, that was a damned good dinner,' said Captain Aubrey, rather loud, as though he were addressing the mast-head. He was not referring to his meal with Sam, though that too had been a capital feast, in the naval style, ending with sublime spotted dog, one at each end of the table, and improbable quantities of port. No: there was a physically far more gorgeous entertainment, a dinner given by the Governor in honour of the Excellency, the Most Reverend Doctor Samuel M'Puta (he kept his mother's name), Papal Nuncio to the Republic of the Argentine, whose government Sam and his father had saved very recently indeed ⊗ — dinner served on gold plate of more than ordinary splendour, with some particularly valued dishes, such as the River Plate lobster served in a bitter chocolate sauce, and some of the finest guinea-pigs ever brought down from the mountains

To be sure, it lacked some of the formal, atmosphere that hovered about a frigate's great cabin, with every guest and servant perfectly aware of the relationship and wholly in favour of the young parson's seamanlike ways & his willingness to drink his wine. Here the connexion, though not unnoticed, was much less obvious, Jack being seated not indeed below the salt but very much nearer to it than his own

He uttered these fine ringing words as he made his way cautiously down the palace steps. Killick & absurdly, Awkward Davis hovering at no great distance — perilous steps: no rail, very sharp edge, deep treads. It was usual to make an inward promise to one's patron saint of a fortnight or even a month's pay before embarking upon them.

AA readily performed
AA slow

Only six steps to go under the high held torches & a small fat boy burst through the crowd and called 'Sir, oh sir: the squadron is in the gut, fast slimming the tide.'

'Thank you, Mr Wells,' said Captain Aubrey: he missed his slip and fell into the Excellency's waiting arms. Davis's prodigious strength supported the double burden: then recovered their balance, and Jack, walking along quite steadily, said 'Sam, I am so very happy. The squadron is stemming the tide in the gut. Even with this breeze they will be here off the island by slack water, and you will see us go aboard. Ho. ho. ha.' Now cut along, there's a good fellow: you must get a decent night's sleep.'

⌐ spyglass folder AA

when a numerous body of infuriated moderates, together with their black followers, defected from those about to break into open rebellion and betrayed their arsenals,

II

The ~~squadron is steaming to hide in the~~ gut. Even with ~~the~~ those they will be moored here off the ~~island~~ by slack water, and you will see us go aboard, ho, ho, ho! Now cut along, there ~~good fellow~~: you must get a decent night's sleep.

A decent night's sleep: there were not many people aboard the frigate who had the least expectation of such a thing. Suppose had only three mast-heads, but all these were firmly occupied by the unruliest ~~most~~ far-off-sighted young men on his books, quite irrespective of ~~rank~~, and they called down every movement together with the ever more portentous news of faintly discerned sail far down in the estuary judged to be the ~~rest of the South African squadron~~ other two squadrons ~~belonging to the common~~ under the authority of the Commander-in-chief of the South African station. The Surprise and her tender Ringle would come under the very close, very knowing inspection of at least two senior admirals, and there was nobody aboard either who wanted her vessel to be moored, sneered at or called a second-hand mud-scow. They wanted no advice on cleanliness, seamanlike appearance, the ~~or the~~ freshening of decks, no facetious observations about their attire; and even the watch below spent most of these precious sleeping time ~~han~~ tidying themselves & the ship. Perhaps the most active was Killick. ~~Ha~~ warrant charged ~~have his magic wardrobe~~ and ~~uh~~ when Captain Aubrey had ~~already~~ served as a commodore, so he already possessed a rear-admiral's uniform: these garments had been a great source of joy to Killick, but an even greater source of anxiety — between in Malaysia, a chandlers' wombat in New South Wales, ~~nameless~~ ~~common~~ from south of the Horn to the tracless wastes of the Kalahari desert had gnawed or attempted to gnaw this superfine ~~unnumerable~~ ~~voracious creatures~~ broadcloth and ~~desecrate~~ the gold lace with their ~~dejection~~. ~~During this anxious vigil~~ with so many of her elegantly scoury

margin left:
a that consolesfactory 50/

arse the balance

the position of the feather is unimportant how is that! moderately sqq.

22 :/

footer: as well as the less authoritative but sometimes even more worrying scrutiny of a large number of officers & above all ratings for precedence and polishing musket cocks. begging much-valued steel from the cook, or (more frightfully) his mates to give the crown-bolts and somethings of a gleam as they lay along in the shot. garlands by the guns — during these active times he sat in the remarkably well-lit space where the surgeons often dissected their specimens or scanned their birds. sat there with Jarvie's best, if rarely-used sea-chest open before him. half its contents spread out on a piece of sailcloth His face was as grave as it could be, and it expressed not only horror but anguish too: for this brilliance showed that his zeal in earlier, much darker times had robbed the cloth of all its bloom. In places it was threadbare: the heap of clothes had something of the sad limp air so evident on Monmouth Street

'Pass the word for Killick' called a voice from the quarterdeck, the second had barrow and the cry was repeated the length and breadth of the ship until it echoed from the open chest itself

'Sir?' he said faintly to the Surgery & captain.

'Have you laid out my number one uniform?'

'Well, in a manner of speaking,' said Killick. 'What it ain't what you might call weatherd very well.'

'Be damned to that.' said Jack. 'It was frozen stiff wear ello wax off the thorn. Just look at my ribbon of the Bath, well you? It sets off an old coat very well'

'Beg pardon, sir' said the officer of the watch. 'Bullock is launching a boat.'

Very true. Her barge was lowering down in a seamanlike manner and manned: her acting-captain took his place in the sternsheets in the stern. They pulled across with particular accuracy and the coxswain brought her alongside with perfectly accuracy.

Captain Simmons came aboard nimbly in spite of his packet

of letters. He saluted the quarterdeck and said 'Good morning sir: I thought you would like these' — holding up his packet — 'as soon as possible.'

'Good morning Simmons — a very good morning to you — how pleasant to see you again. You could not have judged better: we have had no news from home this many a day. Such a welcome packet: thank you very much indeed.'

'Not at all, sir. Do you choose to come back in the Suffolk barge with your coxswain?'

'Thank you: but I think I shall shift my clothes, look through the clerg of these, and then come across at about five bells.'

At the last stroke, he ran down to the sadly washed-over boat where his coxswain was already sitting in the bows with his precious burden, ran down looking very grave. The red ribbon of his order shone in the light as he came aboard the Suffolk: but his face was as grave as ever: there was a profoundly serious occasion and he scarcely saluted as Simmons presented his officer.

The ceremony over, he nodded to his coxswain, standing there by the mizzen, and said 'Heave out the flag.'

The precious bundle soared aloft, followed with intense concentration by all hands: at exactly the right moment, he eased height to a inch. the coxswain snapped the tie and the rear-admiral's blue flag streamed out bravely in the wind, instantly greeted by the fire of thirteen solemn guns, enormously loud, a salutes from all the members of the blue squadron, and distant cheering from Suffolk and clouds of uneasy seagulls complaining

'May I suggest a toast of the flagship, sir?' asked Simmons, with what sauce he could manage, and, together they walked along the decks, with their heavy scent of powder, watched with discreet intensity by all who could decently do so a some who could not.

with its alliance. it intelligent gunner and
his deadly copper-hooped barrels of powder &
touches apron

'Tell me, Simmons.' said Jack as they left the main magazine, walking delicately, as well they might. 'does the Admiral sail with e flag-captain?

'He did.' said Simmons, embarrassed. 'but Captain Fielding is going home with me if Pedrego can find room for us.'

'Ah.' said Jack, aware that his question was untimely. '' only asked because I thought he might answer my less important question — an admiral has plenty to do without being pestered. Perhaps I might turn to his secretary.'

'That would surely answer. Poor Comillet has been hauled over the coals for exceeding his office ... it is very like what you and I knew about Pegasus.

'Oh, indeed?.' That had been a short, unhappy cruise. When Jack was lent to the ship to take the place of her third lieutenant — shot through the head. a ship in which most people seemed to spend their time doing wrong. 'It is not Suffolk I am what's short handed.' asked Jack partly to change the subject but more to learn how a ship of the line could manage with sea so few people. his lower-decks was scarcely populated.

It was a long inspection. and in the course of it Jack met almost all his new officers. a seamanlike set of men upon the whole. and continual welcomings — one or two former shipmates, known long ago. But Jack received a general impression of anxiety and overwork, an impression that was now overlaid by his meeting with the gunner. this matter — Jameset among his lower-deck guns — his 24 lbrs. all or them as heavy cannon can well be and all equipped with Douglas sights.

A long inspection and by the end of it, when they stood there together in the bow, gazing out towards the effectually but still distant squadron Jack had come to love his answer. somewhat heg-udden companion with enough to ask 'Has the heavy weather, have you not found it difficult the ship, so short handed as she is?'.

'I have indeed: and I have heard of it, I assure you ...'

He was cut short by a hail from the mast. head, and a moment later the message came forward: the rear-admiral was desired to go aboard th Flag.

'I am afraid it will be a wet pull,' said Simmons. 'May I lend you a tarpaulin jacket?'

'If you please,' said Jack. His fine but aged uniform had not much wear left in it and he was a long, long way from home

A wet pull it was through an increasingly choppy sea, right into the eye of the wind: it was however shortened by the zeal of the white and the red squadrons to reach a hospitable port

'Well, Aubrey,' said the Admiral, looking at him with a certain satisfaction, 'you have had a wet pull of it, I see. You should have put on an — (as much as his discontented face would allow) — oil-skin. Well, we cannot all be wise all the time. I have called you out so far because there are two questions that I wish to settle. The first is supplies. We are very low in everything — Tobacco is quite gone — and all the way down my porsers, agents and so on have had the utmost difficulty with th locals, even in ports where we have always been welcomed and entertained. ~~Difficulties~~ Difficulties about water, difficulties about coals ... even about common shore supplies — no bum-boats coming off, no whores. What is it like with you in Buenos Aires? Should I push on, do you think? Things are desperate low and with the present ministry in power I dare not use force. How are things with you?

'My lord, until a few days ago we had great difficulties in getting supplies of any kind, but then an eminent ecclesiastic, a Papal Nuncio particularly well known to my political adviser, Dr Maturin ...'

'Yes, yes: Sir Joseph mentioned him to me. I shall pay him some marked attention ..'

'... came in, and now everything is settled. We lack for nothing, and prices are very moderate. We are amply stored for th Cape, and Surprise, which is now bound for home with my dispatches, is in much the same case.'

'I am heartily glad to hear it. That will be a very great relief.' Lord Leyton uttered these words, but his aged yellow face did not match them at all. His expression remained discontented, querulous, readier to find faults or to contradict. However, he did say 'Surprise: yes, that reminds me

(π)

One of the reasons that I asked you to come out here was to tell you that I wished to send two of my officers home in her and to ensure that there should be no trouble about taking them and an unsatisfactory midshipman aboard your vessel.

To be sure I did command her, but 'You will forgive me, my lord, but Surprise is no longer my vessel. She was on hire to the Hydrographical Department of the Admiralty until I should meet your squadron; but my flag and assume my new appointment. The moment I have done that, Surprise's contract with the Admiralty terminates: she returns to the sole ownership of her proprietor, a free agent. If you wish I will ask him if he chooses to take these people aboard: but it is entirely at his discretion. He is at no man's command.'

'What a damned hair-splitting sea-lawyer you are upon my word, Aubrey,' cried the Admiral. 'You can damned well go back to that half-baked privateering donny-forgat, and give the owner my orders to take these two officers and the keeper aboard. If he makes the slightest demur or objection till her shed I shall press every man in his ship and leave him to wallow in the mud of the River Plate until she rots.' At this point the Admiral's yellow face bore on a certain flush and his eyes fairly blazed: one clenched old fist rose & fell.

'The slightest demur or objection … shall press every man …' repeated Jack, rising and drawing her [apron] round him.

'Awkward, legalistic, cavilling sod …' muttered the Admiral: and then, more audibly, as he rang for his steward. 'Sit down, sit down, and drink some madeira to the squadron's supplies. Amphlett' — to the steward — 'the decanter of madeira from the coach: and a couple of glasses. A pause, cried he went on. 'I do not like to see a political adventure to come out in this blue — the Doctor physicked Prince William, did he not?' — but if you would tell him that you have explained the situation and that I should take it as a personal favour if he would [receive] these people aboard his ship.'

'Very good, sir. Now, if I may I shall carry your message to Dr Maturin; [and] if I were to take your [pressing] boat with me in a Surprise, my people could tell them all we know about our [menacesful],

comes to an [illegible]
with
p23

8
π

plentiful sources of supply. The present governor is willing on our side, and I do not think you will be disappointed.

Tomorrow

'Do that thing, Aubrey,' said the Admiral, 'very Well.' 'And when you come to dine aboard me, pray bring your political adviser. I should be happy to make his acquaintance and to offer what civilities I can. [I presume to goes home in Surprise?]'

'Just so, my lord: and indeed I mean to bring to her at once, to transfer some of her hands to poor Old Suffolk. —

'Ay. It was the yellow jack.' of Port of Spain

'And I shall carry your message Your servant, my lord, and thank you for the capital Madeira.

The port back, with the breeze and the sea right aft, and Jack went aboard Surprise in fine style, the side dressed by smiling seamen and officers. He went aboard for the Doctor, who, inured to these ceremonies was reading in the great cabin, reading his letters from home. Jack noticed his serious look, delivered his invitation, and said 'I shall be back in a few minutes: please sort out my post & I shall join you.

On deck he gave the not unexpected order for all hands, and when the particularly attentive group was assembled he said 'Shipmates, as you know, the barky is going home. Some people are uneasy in their minds about being thrown ashore in peace-time.' A general murmur of agreement: intense interest. 'Well, I can take 63 prime seamen with me. Aboard Suffolk it would in course be the same pay, rations & allowances as here, and in her you would find some officers you already know and a score or two of former shipmates. So let them that choose to serve of the South African station give my clerk their names down on a list and I shall mark those I think best suited for the climate.'

A general buzz of strong approval, not quite a cheer, out of respect for a flag-officer, and Rear-Admiral Aubrey plunged off below, where Stephen looked up with a frown, shutting Jack's heap towards him and going on with his own silently.

Sophie Aubrey had almost all the virtues of a woman who had had

MS 9 p 9 is written on the back of π p 6

singularly
2 laid it by a <del>singular</del> ignorant governess → a marvellous history of good kings & bad

very little education beyond the three Rs and a smattering of French.
one who had never been encouraged to read and who in fact had read very
little : but she could and did write a singularly beautiful hand. Her piano-
playing was purely mechanical.. yet on the other hand she was tall. Slim;
her complexion was quite admirable and she moved with a perfect, unconscious
grace — it was a delight to see her going down the dance. <del>but</del> yet she was a
very poor unwilling & horsewoman in spite of arduous. dreaded lessons in
her youth and her husband's kindly. meant encouragement; and she had
never learnt to date her letters

been brought about
not come
Jack's bundle had <del>never been</del> arranged in order <del>of time</del> and although
from <del>they</del> few hints thrown out by chance — <del>&</del> gifts of partridges, the flowers of
<del>birthdays;</del>   certain shrubs, children's holidays — he slowly imposed a remote
<del>hearts</del>   <del>continuance of</del> hint of sequence he could scarcely confide in in it at all
He did make out that his valuable agent was managing his <del>very</del> distant estate
& remarkably well, that the Woolcombe land was more prosperous than
ever it had been and that generally speaking the children's health, apart
from the usual coughs, colds & one greenstick fracture, was all that
could be wished.

<del>He had had a hm</del> The pattern, the history of all that these many
letters told was still very far from clear. but the hint of discord and
unhappiness that he had acquired from the first random letters and that
it had carried with him to the Suffolk — the hint that had much
increased the gravity of that ceremony. now expanded to a conscious
and reasoned certainty: there <del>was so</del> had, indeed been grave unhappiness
at Woolcombe, and in all likelihood there still was

From time to time he glanced over at Stephen, who was earnestly
grave. but whose letters — whose dates and indeed numbered letters — were now
at assembled in neatly ordered piles, that he was now annotating in a
private script as he would have annotated any other body of intelligence
documents.   From time Stephen felt his friend's gaze heavy upon
him; but this was an exceedingly delicate affair. with very strong
emotions involved, and he did not chose to broach a <del>discussion which</del> subject that
concerned Jack even more than it concerned him: still less to force a
confidence.   He said <del>nothing</del> therefore until Jack turned to him

made no observation of any kind

I shall write p 6
& again

and said 'Brother, I am most uncommon slipped today, what
with the emotion of hoisting my flag — hoisting my flag. God bless us
all — and having a set-to with Lord Layton as well as coping
with our people — and I cannot make head or tail of what is going
afoot at home, except that they do not seem such friends. Have
you puzzled it out?' I mean, if you have had the same kind of letters?'

'I believe I have, my dear, though I may well be mistaken. Christine
went down to Woolcombe at my particular request and at dear
Sophie's invitation.'

You will recall

'Yes, yes: I remember it perfectly.'

'At that time your twin daughters were away, at their aunt's
school in Ulster.'

'Just so. They travelled with James Callaghan, whose eldest
girl is there too.'

'So at Woolcombe there were just Sophie, your
young George on long
leave while his ship was being refitted, Christine Wood and my Brigid.
Edward had brought them down from the North Country but at that
point he did not stay, having at least three papers to read before the
Society.'

'All this while we were moving slowly down towards Brazil.'

check

'Perhaps I told you that among a quantity of letters that I received
at Funchal there was a note from Edward speaking of his delight in
the countryside about Woolcombe and his hope of beholding them
one day?'

'Perhaps you did. Do you think that a pot of coffee would
sharpen my wits?' He touched the bell. 'You will take a cup,
I am sure?'

Stephen nodded and went on. 'That was the posture of affairs: a
very elegant posture too, with George & Brigid excellent good friends, often
riding on a stout well-boned pony — the source, alas, of a greenstick
fracture.

'It knit very soon, and it earned him another three months' leave.'

'To be sure. And this was the state of affairs when Edward
came back from London. He had been charmed by the reception of
his papers and he was even more charmed by the countryside; he

R4   93.25

ideal for fishing, for hunting the fox or the hare, and for recording the movements,

11

said he should start making enquiries for a house to be let or sold. observing that although their place in the north was very nice, the weather was exceptionally severe, which his declining health could no longer endure bear. So Sophia, judging very rightly from his coach & carriage, servants and evident style of living, at once suggested a comfortable, fair-sized house not a quarter of a mile away...

'Medenham.'

'Just so... which had been empty for some time, but which, with its gardens & meadows, has been carefully kept up and which was to be had, & at a modest rent by a tenant such as Mr Edward. Woolcombe's own man of business was in charge of the matter, and if dear Mrs Wood liked she would ask him to give them an order to view.

They viewed with every intention of being pleased and they came away delighted. Indeed they would have been difficult to satisfy if they had not liked Medenham, a warm, spacious, low-built house of Charles II's time ago with linen-cupboards to shelter a troop of horses & massive furniture of another age and a considerable library, mostly of natural philosophy.

The affair was soon concluded; necessaries and a few servants were sent down from the north, and the new tenants moved in; the neighbours soon paid their visits, and Mr Edward & his smaller were said to be a great acquisition to the neighbourhood, particularly as Mr Edward spoke eagerly of his intention to hunt that year.

This however proved a hope not easily realized. The horses were there, a handsome bay mare and two promising grey geldings, but Mr Edward had a troublesome neighbour in the north who coveted his estate and when it was refused to be sold turned to the exceeding complex law governing mineral deposits which, he contended, gave him the right to pursue an uninterrupted vein under the adjoining land. Before Michaelmas, therefore, the poor man climbed into his coach again and travelled northwards to his bitter moors through the driving rain, to spend all his diminishing energy in lawyers' meetings and vain attempts at understanding counsel's opinion on the profoundly obscure customary laws of the usage when minerals were concerned in that particular district.

[margin: Instabrems]
During this ~~then~~ Christine spent much of her time at Woolcombe and, except for those necessary hours in the school-room with her new governess, the capable and intelligent Miss West, did Brigid. walking in and out as if it were her own home, often accompanied by her companion George, who sometimes improved his indifferent mathematics with Miss West and sometimes showed both governess and pupil to higher flights of knotting.

[margin: by the barmaster]
It was during the latter part of this season, when field mushrooms were to be had for the picking, that the little household began to look for the return of Mr Edward — he had uttered ~~given~~ some general remarks about having a wheel retyred and the horses shod — when a carriage heard coming up the drive.   For a few moment, those who were drinking tea in the small drawing-room thought it might possibly be Mr Edward's coach, sounding soft because of the rain: but not at all — it was a common post-chaise bringing the twins earlier than usual (not at all uncommon with Sophie's sister, who would seize upon any conveyance, any travelling-companion, to send her pupils home)

The letters that described this home-coming varied, but Stephen, who knew those concerned intimately well, saw the Aubrey girls hurrying in, tired, cross and hungry, intensely jealous at seeing Brigid sitting there by their mother. 'Are you still here?' asked one ~~Charlotte~~. 'You are always here,' said the other, ~~Emma~~ and there was some motion towards pushing her off the sofa,

[margin: strongly repelled by George]
Clearly Sophie and Christine dealt with it situation — the ~~noise~~ clamour of the accompanying ~~sister~~ to bring manservant was a great help — and the Aubrey girls were taken away, washed and fed, while Christine led Brigid home, desiring Padeen to carry the twins' trunk indoors and to settle with postillion

'As I see it, my dear,' said Stephen, 'the twins' jealousy, exacerbated by the weariness of travelling, her eighteen hunger, and the hot squalor of a post-chaise, exploded into real open violence when the same Brigid, peacefully dressed, brushed and sitting in the most favoured place next to the mother,

A good night sleep, a body-bath of warm water, fresh clothes and a substantial breakfast is likely to restore all their amiability.'

'I am sure you are right,' said Jack, but he did not believe it. He knew, far better than Stephen, that there was little amiability to restore. Not from the beginning, when the little girls were virtually one being, but well quite early, he had seen this jealousy directed, at almost any (by a mute common understanding) against any person, any creature even, for whom their gentle and afterwards mother showed a particular liking. Their father, being a sort of household God, was exempt, and so were some of the minor animals; but not George, who was accused of siding with Brigid against them and of running after her too like a little dog.

It was an unhappy state of affairs, above all now that Mr Edward was away in the north and that, Christine was staying at Woolhampton, where her support for ~~in his absence~~ Brigid increased the atmosphere of ill-will.

~~'— fortunately, the end of the holidays is not very, very far away,' wrote Sophie, 'and then they can go back to Ulster, their school where they have such a lot of friends — who are neither prettier nor cleverer or better at French than themselves.~~

'Sometimes I count the remaining days of holiday on the calendar,' wrote Sophie 'They seem to stretch on and on, and I am so afraid that Christine and I may quarrel. Sometimes I see her stop the angry words when the twins are particularly unkind; and rather than have that I am minded to suggest that she and Padeen should travel up to the north to stay with dear Edward, at least until the girls go back to school. I know that she is particularly anxious to escape the attentions, the very pronounced attentions of Captain Miller.'

'I do not think I do know about Captain Miller,' said Stephen.

'He has a moderate estate the other side of Cawley,' said Jack. 'A surprising quantity of pheasants; but a sad coxcomb, I fear. I only say "How d'ye do?" when we meet. A ~~sad~~ soldier, you ~~know~~. He was posted to Sierra Leone at one time.' 'That will be the Admiral.'

he said as the salute began, doubled and redoubled by echoes and by
the citadels prodigious reply to Lord Keyton's civility

'The Admiral is at hand,' said Jack, 'and I should have
told you before that he begs the favour of passage home for his flag-
captain and another unfortunate whose name I forget. I rather
think, brother, that I have pledged your word in exchange for the
recovery of sixty-odd ___ seamen hands to Suffolk, which can
hardly win her anchors else. Oh, they were so happy when ...

'Vittles is up,' said Killick, and the scent of toasted cheese
wafted in with him.

They ate in silence, intently, hungrily, and their sixty less
fork, Jack said 'I have had what I think is an idea worthy
J Newton: but during the night I shall send the rest of my
unless
billes & would they ___ contradict me I shall tell you at
breakfast: for once that is eaten. Surprise must make sail.'

Chapter Three

Chapter III

The diminished but still well-manned Surprise and her lithe fore-and-aft rigged companion Ringle swung easily at their moorings on the making tide, not far from the imposing Suffolk, and they gazed at the South African squadron farther inshore, ardently victualling, watering and getting ready to move into various docks and yards beyond the citadel for repairs, some of them urgent.

'Good morning, Stephen,' said Jack as his friend walked into the cabin.

'Good morning to you, my dear,' said Stephen

'You have done your writing, I see.'

'So I have too: a simple hasty requirement that Brigid shall be delivered into the hands of the bearer to be carried aboard. — whatever vessel she decides upon; this is, I understand, a necessary legal form in case any of Diana's relatives should object. It is, I hope, entirely sotto voce a most affectionate private note to Christine and her brother, inviting them to join us.'

'I have done much the same: simply requesting Sophie to come aboard with the utmost despatch, bringing a minimum of impedimenta, and a course this side.'

Each eyed the other's letter, which looked more like a laboured study than a simple note; & then Jack said 'Well, let us at least have a preliminary cup, & then we can ask Harding to join us.' Some moments later he touched the bell and said to Killick 'Ask Mr Harding to walk in. Mr Harding, pray sit down — may I pour you a cup of coffee?' Now you know very well that Surprise & Ringle are to return to Portsmouth with all possible speed to deliver to deliver a certain number of officers, to to C.-in-C., together with the doctor's messages & my despatches. You may find it possible to shape your course so that you touch at Shelmerston without any impropriety before heading for Plymouth. If it is feasible you, from matured married men, will post straight over to Woolcombe & these hand this letter to my wife, and this to Mrs [?], her new neighbours. Our hope, do you see, is to convey both ladies, the three children,

together with Mr Wood's books.

a close to be a close for their comfort

and the strict minimum of attendants to the Cape, either catching the
squadron before it leaves the River Plate, joining company during the voyage
— we shall almost certainly water at St Helena — or simply at the Cape
itself.   Now you know both vessels through and there; and you know
more than I do about children, attendants and the married state. When
                                                        because it be
you have heard the ladies express their views on these points you will form
an opinion on the irreducible minimum & choose your vessel accordingly.
Ringle is undoubtedly faster than Surprise, but I would not have her
passengers unduly cramped — given a disgust of the sea — for the sake
of a few days.

  'Two ladies, one gentleman, three children, and I suppose three or
or four maids and a man.'

  'It does of course depend upon whether the gentlemen chooses to come.'
observed Jack   'Mr Harding, you will read the letter: they are not in
any way confidential.'

  'I make no doubt that the gentleman will come.' said Stephen.

  Harding, a poised middle-aged man, read the letter with attention.
                                                      at last
The others watched him.   'Well sir,' he said at last   'Well, gentlemen:
I am of opinion that Ringle is the right choice. I were particularly
easy of my sheet when in company with Surprise, though indeed there
are few faster frigates.   They will not be at their ease to be [...]. but they
                                                        to leeward
will have the delight of the bow-wave flung out to the wake racing away,
everything alive & tearing through the water. They would be dull souls as did
not love that; and if I may be so bold. Miss Bridget loved it purely last
time she were afloat in a blow. Anyhow you would want Ringle as a tender.
sir.'

  'Very true: so you think all those people could be crammed in?'

  'I should take my davy on it, sir.'

  'Very well. You can set sail with Surprise, then; and she will deliver
my officers passengers & despatches at Portsmouth, then if run down to be laid
up in Seppings' yard.'

'Very good, sir,' said Harding, folding the letters away in his bosom. 'So now, since the gentlemen to be carried to Portsmouth are already aboard Surprise, I shall ask ^for permission to take my leave and wish you a Surprise & happy, prosperous voyage. And Doctor, how I hope you and your mate will bag a brace or two of phoenixes.'

They shook hands and parted. 'There is a fine fellow,' said Jack. 'He can sail the schooner very, very hard indeed: it was the right choice. But I think he was right when he said they would not always lie at their ease.'

'It would be ill-natured on my part to suggest that he might be influenced by the certainty, under Providence, of coming back to your fine squadron and acting as tender to the imposing great Suffolk under your ^own command: I shall not say it however, although my lower nature does feel exceptionally ill-tempered today. Jack, with your idea you have wholly forestalled me. You spoke of a notion worthy of Newton, but you did not elaborate: and I was only waiting for an opportunity of telling you mine.'

'Pray do so now, dear Stephen: I am sure it would be more luminous.'

'What I was going to say was that you had no idea of the fundamental difference between a landlubber and a seaman.'

'Oh, was you, indeed?'

'You may toss your head in the superior way, but you have never been a mere landlubber. You were ^introduced dipped in the ocean as an infant child; you boxed before you knew the difference between right and wrong; you went positively to sea under Captain Willis well before puberty. Far from you the wondering calf-like gaze of those that watch the embodied machines traverse the Surprise deck — the gaze almost instantly followed ~~by the~~ by the feeling of unavoidable & certain dark, cold death, followed by furious uncontrollable heave and

117

— all this reduces the lubber to state of landsable & permanent monster

III

shameless vomiting, morbid terror and despair. Then, with some slight recovery and even an upright position, the sight of these god-like creatures walking the nightmare deck in these uncouth garments, uttering these brutish cries, hauling upon ropes great & small — finding their way by night — reaching the slimy port! No, no, my good sir, you may say what you please, but there is a great gulf fixed between the land-lubber — the land-lubber who comes late to things that float — and the true born seaman; a gulf as so great as that between a sheep and a seal.

'Very true,' said Jack, who had had the steering of some of the sheep.

'Now you are to consider,' Stephen went on, 'that my Bridget was not only baptized in sea-water, but dipped before she could walk. When we were ashore she rejoiced in boats, when we were at sea & afloat she delighted in heavy seas, never minding in the least when they soaked her through and through — nimble in the rigging, the darling of the upper yardmen. She often explains the rigging to me, & I have seen wise old hands like Tobias nod with approval. No, my dear Jack, what I should have said had you not in essence said it before me, was that one (however young) who has sea-legs, sea-sense, and a knowledge both acquired & to some degree as it were instinctive of the sea's very nature itself, bears down all frippery land-based experience, however old.'

'Oh come, Stephen: Charlotte & what's her name are not exactly crones. As I remember they only date from the Mauritius campaign.'

'They might have been born with Helen of Troy as far as that is concerned. Aboard, particularly aboard so lithe and eager a vessel as Ringle, she must bear them down, and a just equilibrium will be reached, with mutual respect & no bullying.'

There were many vantage points about the harbour that

III

Jack & Stephen climbed once & fairly seasonable time had elapsed, and Stephen had at least the delight of some ~~reasonably~~ moderately upland birds and the breathy mating habits of a colony of variegated scorpions while the sun passed over the almost invariably prime theoretical sky; but Jack made his descent to the still fairly active yards (though his ship was in the last stages of painting) with hope disappointed.

penultimate

Suffolk by now was of a very fine frig, and since Jack was blessed with an experienced, well and upon the whole intelligent wardroom, the gun-crews, at least in dumb-show, were as brisk as he could wish, while the small arms men (who could, within limits, fire their pieces) were well above the average. His stores were of course completed — fine prime salt beef from the immense ranches, water straight from the conduit fed in the mountain, an ~~eminently~~ remarkably agreeable ~~potatoes~~ army biscuit — while for everyday use the fresh-boat plied to and fro, while flat-bottomed craft brought fruit and vegetables in unbounded quantity from the butchers' stalls along the quay. As a peace-maker the Nuncio had worked wonders, though to be sure commercial eagerness had its share.

a smaller quantity of moderate pace

a sudden shower of hail 3rd 99

'It is only a Friday,' said Jack when he and his first lieutenant (he ~~said~~ sailed without a flag-captain) had made sure that there was not a bucket out of place and that all Suffolks were present, correctly shaved and provided with all that was required, 'It is only a Friday, but I think I shall stroll up beyond our usual morning with a telescope. Do you choose to come?'

'I do too: we might see some of the first migrants.'

Up and up: fairly easy going now that they were used to it, and as they took the horizon increased anew enormously, the empty horizon, though in with the land there were some fishermen — lateen rigged.

The mound on which they sat was thinly covered with a sparse herbage, ~~but and~~ in the many bare places the earth showed

he which there grew,
small darkish storm cacline

dull purplish red: a landscape as utterly wholly foreign as
had ever seen. although they had travelled not indeed from pole to
pole but very. very widely — it was often all their cables.

'Dear Lord.' said Jack after a piercing search of the inshore
sea and the northern horizon, 'how I long for Woolcombe. and
this soft green Woolhampton Downs. speckled with sheep. Woolcombe
and the soft new falling. When I was a mere post-captain. you
know, and there was this prospect of peace. I used to console
myself. particularly when I was solvent again with that dear prize-
money and Cousin Edward's land doing so well. I used to console
myself with the thought of restoring the place to what it was when
I was a boy. before my father lost his head about the China Exchange
when we had a pack of hounds and a damned good huntsman, and
the water-bailiff kept the streams as trim as a man-of-war: full of
trout. and the odd salmon in the spring too. Lord. we had such
sport. such fun'. There was an old hound called Captain. and he
always had the line off after a check — they followed him like an
oracle. Lord. how I longed to be back! Now of course I
have to serve my trick as a flag-officer: a most uncommon honour
I am to have it to do. But how I long to be back. sometimes.
under Bramble Down. showing George how to work out a line.
Stephen. you can have no idea how beautiful it is.'

'Can I not?.'

'Oh. of course you can. of course you can. I beg your pardon

I am sure the Glimes d'Avons are even finer   do

'Have you noticed that small vessel right in under the land. almost
beneath us. under the cliff?.'   Her beadle in a line

Jack leapt to his feet. 'By God. she's Ringle.' he
cried. 'She must have stood inshore ....'   the voice and
his explanation died on the downward.   'I should never have
Believed

that a tall man so stout could have moved so fast, said Stephen, fixy
the schooner with his glass. He longed to believe that he could weave out
Christine and Brigid with Edward Heatherleigh clinging to a spar behind
them, but it was clearly time to descend. (35)

The perilous slope, the muskat slope, the bracka-track, the paved road and
at last the Quays with fair-y still far ahead, but moving nearer more than
are admured.

He ~~little~~ Ringle was a beautifully proportioned vessel and it was
only when there was a tight knot of people on her fo'c'sle that one
saw how small she was in fact. Kindly hands heaved a
mooring rope to let Stephen step aboard from the quay and above
over the general din he heard the Aubrey twins' shrill cry, raised
for the seventh time "Why are you not wearing your uniform?"
while at the same time his own Brigid slipped through the throng
and whispered "Dearest Papa," as he bent to kiss her.
Christine was just behind her, and looking at her from the childs'
shums, happy sunburnt face he said "Dear Christine, she does
you infinite credit. Edward, my dear sir, how do you do?"

The visitors' cabins had long since been prepared, and now
the admiral's barge carried them over: after a somewhat cramped
but phenomenally rapid voyage they were amazed by the scale
of a ship of the line — "It is almost as good as Griqua's hotel,"
said Charlotte, which brought her a cross look from Kithra. "And
have you noticed that the sails are ~~square~~ square?" asked her sister, to
which Brigid ~~astonished~~ replied "Don't you ~~even~~ know the difference between a
ship and a schooner?" with such firmness, and in such effect
that Stephen saw, with infinite satisfaction, that his theory had
not been mistaken, that a decent balance had been restored. And
not only that, but Brigid knew quantities of old surprises,* found
them out and asked them how they did, calling them by name,

*some of whom had taught with ropes.

which put her head and shoulders above every passenger but Mrs Aubrey.

[to bottom p 7] Furthermore the twins, as might have been predicted, had been dreadfully sea-sick, confined to their bunks, horrible to see & worse to hear, from the very beginning until a few days ago, so that they had acquired no sea-legs, no fundamental knowledge, so that even now they were & incapable of distinguishing between a rolling-hitch and a bowline.

In a surprisingly short time as it is measured by days, the new inhabitants of the Suffolk, particularly the children, took bells for granted, the silent swallowing of meals, set meals (less Spartan now that they lay in port), the many & very fine gradations that separated the rear-admiral from the boy third class. Stephen observed, with a small but intense satisfaction, that here his daughter, though supported of & sons by Padeen, an old Suspero of remarkable standing said authority had not the least air of being a stranger in the house, a friend's child accepted for that friend's sake: here, with so many friends and accompanied by Padeen, an old Suspero of remarkable standing & authority, and confided with such a friend of sea-going Knowledge she was very much at home. Yet as far as he could see she did not flaunt her sea-going knowledge. But as soon as the twins were willing to be peaceable she was both kind and & companionable.

Very soon they had explored almost every part of the ship from the safest tops (propelled Padeen & other seamen) to the echoing vaults of the darkened hold where facetious midshipmen and first class volunteers would terrify them with sepulchral moans & wavy sheets.

'Dearest Stephen,' said Sophie, passing him a cup of tea in the cabin. 'I cannot tell you how glad I am that our daughters are friends again: there was a time ex at home when I almost despaired — when I should have whipped them if I had not thought it would do more harm than good. It only made me dogged when I was young.'

'I cannot imagine you being whipped, Sophie,' said Christine.

'But I *was*, and Cecilia often too. My mother would make us stand with our faces to the wall and whip the back of our legs with a scourge made of willow-wands: I do not think it ever improved my French verbs or arithmetic or even "manners".'

'I knew some Dominican nuns who did that,' said Stephen. 'They whipped my Saavedra cousins until they bled: I had supposed it was only Catholic. Jack hardly ever flogs: discourages it, indeed. How do you find him, my dear?'

'Oh, very well. I *thank* you,' said Sophie, blushing. 'I must admit he is rather sterner than I could wish: but he does look harder, less flag, and I am so very very happy for him. It was Prince William who sent us the news, with his best compliments, which I thought was wonderfully polite.'

The other three little girls came in, since if there was tea there might also be, in the nature of things, be cake, or at least muffin. On seeing Stephen they stopped, not looking very nice, and the two made a concerted bob; then Brigid ran over to him and said Oh sir, the Admiral says a Portingee came in with the flood and he hopes there may be some mail. A boat pulled across to the flag,' not long since.'

'I shall go upstairs — I shall go on deck, and ask whether it would be proper to exercise. Ladies, forgive me, I beg.'

No. It would be most improper. Jack were surprised that a man who had seen so much sea-time could suppose such a thing possible or even decent — it was not exactly mutinous but it would deserve and most receive an exceedingly bitter reproval. But in any case Stephen was talking great nonsense. The Portingee had been aboard Lord Leyden this hour and more and there

10 ∓

nothing carried up the side,

is no sign of mail — no handing out of bags, no hurrying to and
fro. No. The boat had done nothing more than deliver the gentleman
the gentleman in regimentals who is walking up and down the quarterdeck
with the Admiral arm in arm. I have been staring at him with my
glass in this ill-bred fashion for some little time. for although I think
I know the face I cannot put a name to it. Will you take a look?

'Sure, it's very ill-bred: but I might, to you make you easy.' He
took the telescope, focus focussed. and almost at once. as the wise
men on the far ship learned. he said coldly. 'It is Henry Miller.
He was at Trinity and he killed Edward Toaffe in the Fifteen Acres when
I was in my last year.

'Miller? Yes: that is Lord Leylan's family name. Then meant to
You. of course, my neighbours over by Caxley: he must be related
to the Admiral — Miller is Lord Leylan's family name. and the man
I know often spoke of a peerage going to some fairly close connexion
cousin. of course. they would not be walking arm in arm, else.'
After a pause face went on. 'He killed a gunner in a duel in Malta
too. He is said — obviously, to be a very good shot, with capital
pistols: I have heard him called Hair-Trigger Miller, and to be
sure I have seen him bring down a great many pheasant.'

'Would you say he was a quarrelsome man at all?'

'I scarcely know him. We are nosecases acquainted, but to do to
he is not the kind of man whose acquaintance I should value—
in short I do not like him. It is not the frailty. Such as
much more usual in the army than with us. as you know. and
anyhow we have took him out from time to time.

11

Jack stood over the water and went on.

'For all I know he may be well enough liked in his regiment. But his reputation in the neighbourhood is so indifferent that I was surprised to learn that he had called on Edward and Christine when they settled in Medenham. And then at Woolcombe when Christine was staying there with Edward so busy in the north. I have no room to blackguard a man for incontinence. being no model myself; but there are limits... You know very well. Stephen, how much influence a of man with a large household and a considerate extra can bring to bear on his dependants — his dependants' daughters — and there were some very ugly tales of girls in child being turned away.' 'I know very little. Yet his conduct does seem to match with the general reprobation.'

'He is not married. I take it?'

'No. Not ever has been. Since he is next in succession to Leyton title, he is said to be saving himself up for some very brilliant match.'

'Can you square a man's valuing a peerage very highly with his going out and risking his life so often?'.

'Yes. If he is an unusually resentful creature and at the same time a very good shot.'

'Sir. if you please.' said the officer of the watch, stepping aft and taking off his hat. 'Flag is breaking out a signal.'

Speaking in the high staccato, expressionless voice usual on such occasions midshipman piped up 'Flag to Suffolk: Admiral invites Rear-Admiral and Doctor MATURIN to dinner at . quarter past three. repeat a quarter past three.'

'Rear Admiral to flag: very happy.' said Jack in richer & freer. speaking more like a human being. 'Pass the word for the Doctor. Stephen, (in a pierced tone. and then leaning over the taffrail) I have engaged you to dine with the Admiral tomorrow: I hope you do not mind it?'.

'I do not mind it. my dear; and it would make no odds if I did. We are all worms under the harrow, in the service. even you.

standards indeed. The being both steady and favourable
Jack had laid on his favourite, most profitable form of exercise, one
calculated to promote zeal, speed, & above all accuracy, to unite
a gun-crew into an immensely active cooperation while - never a word
passing, never a word called for - and to promote the most valuable
sort of competition. The most experienced gun-captains and the older,
more midshipmen were at the three forward guns; and bitter shame would
fall upon any following gun that could not keep up well with them in speed
or accuracy.

The first three guns had been ordered to fire high, to leave sufficient
for the rest of the broadside; and Jack, as a particular, went
silences or gob-stopped for the little girls, had with the quarter-
master, contrived a flimsy but coherent structure that under very
light and warm net canvas would drift overhead until it was abreast
of the man-of-war, which would then pound it with the most
rapid broadside compatible with Sophie's timbers - rolling, but only just
rolling.

'Target's away' hailed the forecastle lookout. 'On deck there
Target's away.'

'From forward as she bears' called Jack, and there was a
long, tense silence, broken only by the gentle wind in the rigging.
The little girls, in white frocks, stood a tip-toe: just behind them Sophie
and Christine, almost equally tense. The captain of Number One
glared along his sights, his lanyard in his right hand, his left making
very slight delicate movements to swivel or elevate the heavy gun-barrel
right or left, up or down a trifle. Fire! he cried and heaved
on the lanyard: the hammer shot forward and with barely the least
perceptible pause the gun uttered its profound roar, a great jet of smoke
and flame enveloping the cannon-ball and the racing gun-carriage and
barrel racing inboard with a screech of trucks under the arched bodies
of its crew until the whole was brought up short with a great twang

by the tackles: but already there were immensely active hands clearing away any smouldering remnants from the guns, swabbing the barrel, ramming down the next charge of powder. On the deck, then the wads well chumped down, and barely pausing for the breech seeing the whole mass upon up against the side which the captain pierced and primed his own, unmoved by the truly appalling rocking of his neighbours as he and his mates made all fast and levelled the warm gun again

The firing went clear down the battleships side at a few time even pace, and even the aftermost piece had its shot at the final remnant that drifted by. But by then the little girls had almost no voice to screech nor even the emotional power to do so: the enormous and repeated din, the vibration of the ship and the air, the great flashes and a dense cloud of smoke drifting away to leeward had overpowered them; and the near-stupefaction of their elders was very impressive too. Sophie had seen sloops & moderate frigates at gun-exercise but never a ship of the line, and she was much remarkably preserved not only by the unconscionable din but extremely more by the reflection that this was what her profession subject her husband to. Christine, to be sure, had fired many and many a fowling-piece and even a rifled gun on occasion, but nothing imaginably on this scale, and she yet remained quite mute, holding Brigid's hand, until after a good deal of calling out right forward the cry came down. 'On deck. On deck there. Target's away, sir.'

from a earlier version as a readers

So it was, a great long raw-sheaved affair of all sizes of old casks and nameless objects clapped together and furnished with every cloth of a sort to carry its whole downwind. The target appeared on the starboard bow, towed by boat that cast off as soon as they it was well on course. An active intelligent master's mate ran down the broadside 'No fire until the admiral gives the word: then count

count two between each shot.'

A profound silence: the target drifted half way down the gunboat's length. 'Fire.' said Jack.

The first gun: and before it quite rang in the second and so close along the line down to the last. When the smoke cleared and the last repeated echo died away there was nothing but Joseph's voice to be seen. The little girl had strength enough to utter a last gasping Oh. and they were led away exhausted: but not before a furious Killick had appeared on the quarterdeck waving a full-dress coat. 'Which I had it all laid out a quarter of an hour long dead. Ain't you got ...' He was going to say 'No shame?' but unapproving looks, coupled with Jack's instant compliance and a call for the barge checked his text.

With a following breeze and a very well inclined crew the barge fairly skimmed across the sea. hooking on only a muller of seaman lace. In any case Lord Leyton was in a good mood - he could be jovial and he could be damned crabbed - but this was a good day. He had heard most of Dr Maturin's acquaintance, close acquaintance, with the Prince William. the Duke of Clarence. who, in view of his elder brother's constitution, was likely to be king in the fairly near future. 'Well Aubrey.' he cried, giving his guest a hand as he came aboard. 'You very nearly split this heavens with that damned great rolly broadside — Gad in my life. thunder and lightning was nothing to compare. Don't I wish you may not have stove more than of a dozen of gun limbers. he. he. ha! And don't I wish you may have come by your powder honestly. ha. ha. ha. ha! Allow me to present my young cousin Randolph Miller — beckoning to a soldier in regimentals, smiling just behind him — teal of colour you know him already, you are neighbours in the country..

'How do you do. Sir?' said Jack. taking Miller's proffered
accepting

two between each shot.

A profound silence: the target drifted half way down the Suffolk's length . . . 'Fire,' said Jack.

The first gun and before it quite seen in the second and so clear down to the last: and when the smoke cleared and the last repeated echo died away there were nothing but some loose wreck to be seen. The whole gun had strength enough to say a last gasping Oh. and then they were led away, exhausted: but not before furious Killick appeared on the quarterdeck waving a full dress coat. 'When I heard it all [?] out a quarter of an hour too fast. And you got . . . ' He were going to say 'no shame.' but disapproving look, coupled with fair compliance and his call for a barge checked his zeal. //A

The barge fairly raced over the smooth water with the incoming tide and they were not perceptibly late, and in any case Lord Leyton, willing to be affable before Dr Maturin, of whom influence with the Duke of Clarence he had heard strange things, greeted them pleasantly enough. 'By God, Aubrey.' he said 'you fairly split the heavens with that last rolling broadside. Don't I wish you may not have started more than a score of your timbers; and may I read you came by your powder honestly. he, he, he. Dr Maturin. how do you do. sir? Prince William spoke most kindly of you when last we met. Said you were most uncommon clever. May I introduce him my cousin. Captain Miller - though now I come to think on it, perhaps a physician takes rank over an army officer?'.

'How do you do, sir?' asked Stephen, bowing. And the how do you does were repeated by Jack and Miller and some other guests as they made their way, often giving preference, to the Admiral splendid. Eight they sat down. and with the servants behind each chair they were by no means crowded. Jack, as a flag-officer sat at the Admiral's right, with his Admiral's cousin opposite. 'I hand.

'And this, sir, is Dr Maturin, I presume?' said LдL. 'How
kind of you to come. I have had a particular desire to see you
ever since the Duke of Clarence told me that you were a most
uncommonly to learned man. I am not particularly learned
myself, but I love to surround myself with those that are. May
I pre introduce you to ^{Capt H.} my cousin Randolph — but now I come
to reflect, perhaps the doctor of medicine takes rank over a
soldier...'

'Not at all, my lord: but it so happens that we were at
Trinity College together, so I already have that honour.'

'So he was. Trinity College, Dublin. So if he too were at
Trinity, he too is one of the learned: it stands to reason. And
may I introduce...'

Presently they were called to <del>dinner</del> ^I dare say he is splitt you
an of introduction as much as
any man
of the Admiral's truly splendid dining-cabin, which could sit people
easily, with a servant behind each chair and plenty of room
for those who came hurrying in with dishes and tureens. sauceboat
trays of bread, and of or course very large quantities of wine
— a grateful Sancerre with the bonito, <del>a dressing</del> ^on Kant. Baron with the admiral's
duck, and a burgundy of an outlandish year with the roast
beef: unhappily, it was corked. The chaplain, to stephen right
murmured something about 'a quaint odour of antiquity,' and they
did not empty his glass; but their host did not notice his first
sip and none of his officers showed any sign of awareness.
'Stoics?' asked asked Stephen privately 'Duchess of Athenay.
great man? Stoics inexorably?'

When it came to the port, however, the case was altered:
all hands, including the parson, drank eagerly; and when it
came to the loyal toast there was no man who did not raise
his brimming glass and murmur 'God bless him,' with real feeling,
having emptied it.

III

17

After the ceremony and the chaplain's grace, Lord Leyton observed that although the glass was sinking it was still a very fine afternoon, and some of them might like to take their coffee and perhaps some brandy, on deck

There were general sounds of agreement, a general movement though with due regard to precedence, and the Admiral keeping Jack by his side until the room was free, said, in answer to his thanks and congratulation 'Not at all, not at all, my dear fellow - a very simple little feat. Though I must admit that they have capital band here. But did you notice anything about the burgundy?'.

'No, sir: capital wine.' excellent

'Well, I am glad of that. For a moment I thought - but, however, what I wanted to tell you before coffee is that I should like you to weigh in the ebb and to proceed to S Helen, under a very easy sail, there to wait in that damned uneasy Roadstead until you see me clear. Then you must weigh and carry on for the Cape. there is not room for all of us squadron to lie there safely together in, any some weather. But that will already mean a very impressive show of force.'

'Certainly, sir.'

'And then I should like you to take my nephew along with you. As you may know, he certainly has been an apprentice at the Cape, and the sooner he is there the better - you might even lend him your tender for the last few days. Now let us hurry on deck, before all these God-damned soldiers have drunk all the brandy'

On deck Captain Miller at once came up to him and said 'Sir, I hear with great pleasure that Mrs Aubrey and

17a

This will go
at the end of
MS III 17

For the Cap.

'You will carry on still under a fairly easy sail, and I
make no doubt that we shall overhaul you a little south of
Capricorn — at all events well before Loando, where I mean to
put in so that we may all reach the Cape together in full fig.
And from that point on I should like you to take my cousin
along with you. As you may know, he has an appointment at the
Cape, and the sooner he is there the better: you might even lend
him your leader for the last few days, so that he can report
promptly and snap up our say the best houses before there
is any competition. Now let us hurry on deck, before these
God-damned soldiers have drunk all the Brandy.'

He moved briskly up the ladder and right aft where a graceful
breeze was wafting from the ocean — As soon as Jack had followed
him into the open air he was accosted by Allen, who took his arm
and said 'Sir it is with the greatest pleasure that I hear that Mr
Aubrey and Mr Wood are both aboard again. and it is
not impossible that perhaps we may be shipmates as far as the
Cape.' He came back carrying the brandy and turn to Melano
he cried. 'Yes, my dear cousin tells me that you will be so very kind
as to tene us with you after the squadron has refreshed at Loando,
and I thank you very very much indeed. I did myself the
pleasure of waiting on Mr Heatherleigh when he and his sister - whom
I already knew well, and admire from my days in Sierra Leone —
were selling at Medenham; and oft later I called on Mr Aubrey and
Mr Wood at Woolcomb when you were shut at sea — I must
congratulate you on your children sir!

Jack looked at him with some surprise. Their degree of acquaintance
did not warrant anything like this familiarity. Has the fellow
drunk too much? he wondered inwardly. aloud he said 'Forgive me if you

Mrs Wood are both aboard you, and that perhaps we might
shipmates as far as the Cape. Allow me to fetch you, a glass of
brandy.'   He came back, carrying it and cried 'Here.
How's my dear cousin to tell me that you will be so very kind as
to take me with [thank you very, very much indeed.   I did
myself the pleasure of waiting on Mr Heatherleigh when he and his
sister – whom I already knew and admired from my days in
Sierra Leone – were settled at Megueakeam; and, little later
called on Mrs Aubrey and Mrs Wood at Woolcombe when you
were still at sea.'   I must congratulate you on your children, sir.'

you after the
signalmen has
put in to board

Jack looked at him with some surprise. Their degree of acquaintance
did not warrant anything like this familiarity. 'Had the man
drunk too much?' he wondered uneasily, and went he said
'Forgive me if you please.' and he walked over the deck to
where Dr Maturin was listening sullenly to Lord Leyton's harangue –

and parentitts

a detail detailed explanation of how he was going to tell Napoleon
how he could have avoided defeat at Waterloo.   'Aubrey'
he cried, turning. 'Cannot you persuade or even order Dr Maturin
to stay which I have my interview with the Emperor – with

Ian B

Napoleon, I should say. I can read the French pretty well
with a dictionary, but I cannot really speak it –'

   'Oh come, my lord.' said Stephen. 'What you say sounds fa
very like the French of the northern provinces; and I do assure
you I have patients aboard the when I own my first duty, to
say nothing of what awaits me at the Cape –

   'My lord,' said Jack, 'even an admiral cannot oversule
a medical man – it is in the Articles of War – and even if
he could he would have no success with Maturin. You may
take a bear from his vomit, but I do solemnly affirm that

capitulation?

the First Lord of the Admiralty could not turn Malcolm from his set course, perverse though it may be. But here is my teeth and the barge is alongside: I thank you very heartily indeed for your hospitality, and I shall most willingly carry your nephew to the Cape. Good day to you, my lord. Comr. Stephen.

An admiral's barge, though spacious, is still a public place, and they said little as they returned to the ship:

> No: I shall have to rearrange
> these pages of on the typewriter

> And I must remember to tell the girl
> about my missing shoes

> If I go back to & TCD I might
> look for pen-cartridges

> what shall I do with him?

19

ten beats of the largest curve could not deter Madren from what he thought right. And I do assure you your lordship that when we have some people on the sick-list in a very parlous state.'

'How do you d mean - pet parlous?'

'Well, my lord, nip and tuck, as you might say, or touch and go. And it is my impression that as soon as his assistant Dr Jacob comes aboard he means to operation operate on a strangled hernia.'

'A twisting of the guts, my lord: the front-sort, swelling above because his strangulated feel him twice at every meal; and he shrunk below. The patient is a sailmaker's mate.'

'Well, I am sorry for him, but I am sure to have nothing to recover but a double handful of small-sho followed by a pint of castor oil. Yet it is really a medical's business & I shall certainly leave it to. It Would it be a very bloody affair?'

'Shockingly so, I fear; though with clips & swabs we shall try to diminish the flow.'

'I might mention it to Madren. He watching wishes to see the castration of lambs and bullocks. — geldings, for that matter.' The Admiral gave a something like the full Trady, clear of the land and its circumstances said th Admiral, and he ... the little ... himself ... some full and strong ... a ... You will have ... go ... to year old Suffolk and perhaps you ... so many ... their ...

presently he formed the whole South African Squadron into the sailing order, sending his guests back to their ships in the kindest manner.

Truly, once they had sunk the land it was the purest sailing: nearly 300 miles in its full day, never touching tack nor sheal, and even the Suffolk kept in splendth. How bitterly would them keenest navigators Heaven and Damnd, who would so have loved drawing the almost purely straight lines cutting the parallels at even angles. But how then expunged these occasional northern albatross, the not unfrequent whales, the almost steady accompaniment of quite a large variety of shares and even rays!

Jack Or   's twins began to grow rather observant, knowledgeable about sea-going affairs but Padeen (to his delight remained strange, incorrect and largely incomprehensible for the finer points) managed to keep them within bounds, and what he could not do Borgia did. It did not make them very pleasant companions but it rendered them tolerable; and the southern coast of Africa and its Portuguese possessions came daily nearer

Miller, who called on the ladies almost every day to suggest piquet or backgammon (with little success after he whist) was much excited by the prospect of Loando, and he climbed as far as dared to catch a first glimpse of the shore — conceivably a symbol of power, status and indeed perhaps marriage

A dinner on the western horizon, soundings, very exact observations of sun, moon, planets, and a wonderfully timely eclipse of one of Jupiter's satellites gave them their line to the minute or ever less

'Now it can come hell or high water' said Harding, the Suffolk's first lieutenant and a postmaster. Now you know exactly where we are.

He said this in Captain A the presence of Admiral Aubrey (no mere astronomer himself) who shook his head at the words: so did everyone else in the chartroom, sometimes imperceptibly. But imperceptibly or not, within seconds the sky split into a most enormous roar — so prodigious that the twins, well accustomed to seatime weather, rushed shrieking into their mothers bee

All night it followed and threatened St Helena's Fox appeared of on many separate, and the bowsprit three croyent were blown out of their foll, toper in the first shout, and the foll topgallant. With infinite pain. On a deck that never for a moment stopped heaving manner

slowly along about in the most extravagant manner, they stowed all that could be stowed and then turned to the pump for the very serious mass of water still below, and to plain swab and bucket for the knee-deep wet that washed from side to side of the sick-berth. the captain's cabin and the lieutenants store-room

A heavy day night, with nothing to eat but wet biscuit & rum; but it did clear before dawn and rising sun showed not only a beautifully clear but the coast of Loanda. with its town and its bay. The sea was still grievously troubled and there were half a dozen fishing-boats at least half-wrecked or worse. The South African squadron as a whole had taken to very early in the night — their topsail were above the horizon, — So Suffolk picked up the fishermen, & towing their boats carried them into Loanda, having signalled his intention to the squadron

They were most lovingly received — many of the fishermen were relatives and they were feasted (though at short notice) in the most splendid, while as far as the exhausted hands were concerned went down very well indeed. The Admiral commanding squadron was housed in a rapidly brushed governor's: the nominal which squadron had no flag-officer at its but Jack who was after all a rear-admiral of the blue, lived with all his family and senior officers, in the former military command, next to still not inconsiderable barrack

In spite of the shortness of the storm the ships had suffered extremely and he, Jack and the other captains were almost perpetually in the well-equipped and capable dockyard. One day, as they were coming back to the Governors house — a shingle strand with singularly coconut palms and their usually birds — Stephen met them and the Admiral asked after his heroics.

'Thank you. sir.' said Stephen. 'he has shown the most remarkable improvement and I think I shall operate in the next two days, now that Jacob is returning. Perhaps I shall mention it to Captain Miller.

'Yes. maned: he loves medical matters. Bullet is not particularly is it?

'Oh, no. Nothing like an amputation. You open intelligently and you are on the job at once.

'Well, in that case it would be very kind of you, I am sure.'

Stephen came carried on to the military headquarters, and when in he found Milleif already there, not to his surprise although it was an almost daily occurrence, but surprising in the way the bunches of flowers had increased and in Christine marked infavourable ~~extreme~~ expression

'Oh Captain Miller,' he said, accompanying him to the door, 'I happened to tell the Admiral that I were probably operating upon ~~too~~ a favourite of her's to-morrow. Should you like to attend?

'Is it a bloody operation?'

'Oh no. Not what one should really really bloody. If your first incision is badly mistaken it can be somewhat distressing, but we do not usually mistake'

'I am sure you do not. But if I may I will excuse myself for these occasions though with many many thanks for your polite attention.'

'Good day to you, sir.'

'Stephen, my dear,' said Christine, 'I am afraid I must beg you ~~till~~ to tell that man not to call unless he is invited. It is because quite a nuisance — a wonderfully confident nuisance. He spent a long time in telling me though all this & even and telling me that when he had taken up his appointed position at the Cape and when he had married to woman he had chosen there would be virtually nobody in the colony to compete with him in wealth and influence. I have met with some fools in my life, even some God damned fools, and a good many of them; but I have never met with such a confident ass as Miller: I suppose he view of his view

& completely blinded by his position, appointment and I dare say
wealth, as well a gross stupidity. Stephen, please get me rid of
him. He is making his relations as well as himself.

'My dear, I shall attend to.'

It was when the South African squadron was fit for sea that the
Admiral ordered them to sea, there to carry out a very considerable
great-gun exercise fairly close in shore to the please their Portugese
friends. The last preparation had not yet taken place before Stephen
Maturin met of of Captain Miller. 'O Captain Miller,' he said
& detaching himself from his friends. 'I have message for you. (low
his voice) Mrs Wood begs you will not call again with an invitation.'
Miller could not a first grasp the meaning. though his complacent
smile did fade. Stephen repeated his words.

'It is not true,' cried Miller. 'Christine never said that.'
'I assure you those were her words.'
'There were not &'
'You give me the to lie?' asked Stephen, very low. approaches his face.
'Yes,' cried Miller, and struck him hard. (who had rejoined
a little after midnight)

'You will appoint your friends,' said Stephen. 'These gentlemen —
nodding towards Harding and Joseph, will attend to my
interests. Good day to you, sir. until early tomorrow morning.' He
touched his hat and walked on.

Harding was obliged to leave them to buy some particularly choice
handkerchiefs for his wife. and Stephen said 'Oh my dear Jacob,
how sorry I am to entangle you with that silly little affair even before
you have answered half your questions on your most admirable report
of the Argentine. Shall we have time for a small well-placed
uncomplicated heroic & before going deeply into practice?
I should have to get word off to Sir Joseph directly since we must sail after
early tomorrow afternoon

'I should imagine so - really hostile, less patient next a simple heroic
is no great matter and I have already coded the essence of my report.
And a simple affair of this kind is no greater matter either: small enough

o blow seven & remember

on the level ground behind the groyne, c. half a mile seaward, we put a soldier. his men and a local surgeon. You expect no serious injury?

'No. A grazed shoulder at the most'

'Very well. Let us look at our patient & perhaps operate at once, or at the ? seat of landing him until the execution is over.'

In fact, although the operation went perfectly well. the man Hawkins was landed at the Admiral's particular request. on two grounds: the first that it stood to reason some gun or other would burst or overset, and second, that the roaring of broadsides would rouse his feeling & excite the blood; whereas ashore he would be perfectly calm and well under Mrs Aubrey's & Mr Wood's care.

But the Admiral was worried, very much more worried. by his ... nephew as serve in the marines and by his rumours. brought by a Admiral's secretary that Miller had flatly refused to fight with a sloop. He would pistol or he would not fight. Maturin's second would have none of it: it was their principal who had been struck – it was he who chose the weapons. That was always the case: it always had been the case. It was the Law of Moses

'Of course it is.' said the Admiral. 'I always preferred the gentleman's weapon who I went out: except when I was the aggressor and had to take the other man's choice = Pray, Mr Martin.' he went on. 'pray turn out & see if you can catch them. Tell his private friend that if he don't fight he is disgraced for ever & can expect no notice from me – no frank divinity ☉ And tell me a sword wound wound given by a reasonably decent creature is not so wicked. particularly if ? dress it with marshmallow and heartsease.'

the few v e of

On the field. from which so ... onlooked had been showed with appalling violence, the scene was only just not ridiculous Miller had been urged forward by his seconds and he kept telling them that it was perfectly unfair – he knew everything about pistols; he would meet any man with a pistol. But he knew nothing about a swords

They. stone-faced. kept telling him it was the law of the duel. He could either apologize on his knees, using any terms his adversary saw fit to impose. or he must fight. There was no true ways about. Mr Martin whispered into his ear "Your uncle will not speak to you if you do not fight"

They thrust a sword into his hand, pointed ~~by~~ toward that of his adversary. The chief second held them on his outstretched blade. cried 'Gentlemen engage,' and stroke back

Two. three or even four clashes. and Miller's flaw cut to act. It landing between them. Stephen put his ~~a~~ foot on it and his ~~past~~ sword-point against. 'Do you withdraw?' he asked. 'Miller, do you withdraw your words entirely?' 'I do. Entirely.'

'Yes?' Then we have said enough. Good-of day to you, gentlemen ~~heartily~~ and I thank you for ~~for the~~ your presence

'He ~~forsooth~~ showed all with a set of toasts,' said Wainwright into Killick's eager ear. He was Miller's servant and he cordially disliked his master; but since he was a child and grandchild of Colley Horns he had ~~to~~ learnt to express himself in gentler expression — not that there had any other currency whatsoever with Killick or nine. tenths of the lower ~~de~~.
'Where does he slow himself now?'

'Why. in the little cabin behind his lordship; and I doubt he comes out ~~of~~ so soon. ~~But~~ It is fair wonderful what a face of brass will do, but I doubt anyone could face this country — the English country. the past ~~are~~ around us, or in London — having as it were as damnit refined to fight I remember how his Lordship went out half-dozen times when I was young_ and always bloodied his sword... Come-ee' he cried. and vanished oft.

Killick delighted in pineapple-short and in frog's trotters; but they did not nearly reach his high and exalted pleasure in very specifically ~~obscene~~ obscene (which alas he could never remember accurately or even at all) stories, however improbable and accounts of high life

He did not come on deck the next day, that of the *prodigious, lengthy* very
naevey great gun exercise; nor did he appear for the smallarms exercise
in which he had trained some of the Marines. From time to
time he turned into the wardroom when almost nobody was there. His
appearance never altered perpetually (a pen or a newspaper) from its purolled smallpox
complexion, yet he frequently changed his uniform, blamy he probably
stroot for any nap

Some days of clear untypical Baptist St S Africa upsetten weather
showed the squadron and it was possibly during these hours
sitting in the cabin that possible and it was with him
her during the conversation

15
TSS

No: there is still a lot of III — LdL's dinner or part of it — *recon*
It is not in the MS before: but I remember now that there was a
table-plan in the lowest margin

Alas. I cannot find it: LdL pages have lost *off* MS chapters
on the almost daily basis of my life: could there be a
malignant hard hand?

In this case I may be able to rebuild the odd pages: But
I shall have to do first and concentrate what wits I still possess

£ JA pulls *sgr* across barely leg

LdL big elderly interested jovial 'split th heavens'
interested in SM's friendship with Clarence — transmute phrase
— present Capt Miller "my cousin

Ó sheen
& I think

(seating)   Miller over-familiar   *comes 2nd*   *message Jacob*
                                   at coffee   *to whisper? St J is aboard
                                                  pretty spry but rather Wo*

LdL

JA   Miller
              Flag capt
senior RM
(col? Major)

SM

Dr W

Chaplain

(I must read through for
names of ships)

& work out Suffolk's
wardroom

afterwards privately
LdL asks JA to
proceed down to St Helena
under easy sail, taking Miller
(who has an *appointment* secondary
appointmt at th Cape) & to
lie off in the intellectual holding ground
& as soon as sails are seen to Weig
(show of force)
perhaps as some of the squadron
are dull sailers Miller might be lent
tender (? name)

Afterword by Richard Snow

The other day I heard Patrick O'Brian receive about as high a compliment as a writer can get. An old friend of mine, a professor of history and literature, had just read *Master and Commander* again for the first time in a decade. "How well it holds up!" he exclaimed. "It's amazing. That first meeting, it's like –" He waved his hand as he searched for a comparison. "It's like Prince Hal meeting Falstaff."

The meeting, of course, takes place between Lieutenant (for just a few more hours) Aubrey, and a weedy-looking little physician named Maturin. It was a contentious meeting, and might well have led swiftly to the death of one of the two – most likely the young naval officer. Instead, of course, it led to the greatest friendship of modern literature, and ushered millions of twentieth-century citizens into a world warmed and clouded by sea-coal fire, rationalized and tormented by the architects of the Enlightenment, fed salvers of steaming offal washed down with suicidal quantities of claret and port, and defended by hundreds of close-packed seaborne towns whose elders' grasp of mathematics, physics, ballistics, and meteorology was all that stood between the residents and extinction.

My friend who made the Shakeseare comparison, Fredric Smoler, had come early to this harsh, seductive world, back when its creator's books were struggling to find an audience in the United States. Lippincott, Stein & Day, *Master and Commander, Post Captain, HMS Surprise* . . . the publishers tried and withdrew – after *Desolation Island*, permanently. Or so it seemed. During the years of drought, Patrick O'Brian's acolytes did what they could to keep Jack Aubrey and Stephen Maturin in their lives. They opened accounts at the great English bookstore Hatchards; they wrote to booksellers in Canada; the most fortunate of them acquired, along with the precious novels, a correspondence with the lively and generous-spirited Richard Ollard, O'Brian's English editor, and himself a formidably accomplished historian and a superb writer. Another friend of mine, the journalist Mark Horowitz (who would later publish an influential profile of Patrick O'Brian in the *New York Times Magazine*), had left New York to become a belligerently loyal Angeleno, and sent Fred and me messages saying that every bookshop in Los Angeles stocked imported O'Brian novels – and how do you like that, you haughty Manhattanites? (Surely this can't have been entirely true, and yet Mark always seemed to have read the latest one before we did.) In the meantime, of course, we proselytized, with the predictable success:

Them: I've read all the Hornblower novels, and that's enough for me.

Us: But that's like saying, I've read *Robinson Crusoe* so there's no reason for me to look at Dickens.

Such harangues often ended with an indulgent smirk from the victim. And why not? If this writer was really all that good, everybody would know about him, right?

It's a fair question, and eventually Starling Lawrence answered it. He is the editor-in-chief of W. W. Norton & Company, and in 1990 O'Brian's agent, Vivien Green, pressed a copy of *The Reverse of the Medal* on him as he was leaving London bound for New York. By the time he disembarked at JFK he had been won over: he would bring out the next O'Brian, *The Letter of Marque.* This was a courageous decision; the series had already failed here, and it is considerably more costly to publish a writer than it is to pester your friends about him across a dinner table.

But it turned out to be the right time. All those scattered little enclaves glowing with O'Brian enthusiasm were ready to reach combustion. The resulting blaze created rather than destroyed; so far it has cooked up five million copies and an admirable motion picture that will continue to spread the word for years to come. (That the movie became the object of some prissy reproach for not more fully unfurling the characters of Stephen and Jack only ratifies the power of the books that gave it birth.) This American enthusiasm sent ripples back across the Atlantic. On a visit to London in the mid-1990s, I was gratified to see that O'Brian's novels had been moved out of "Naval Fiction," a bookstore section we alas don't have over here, across the aisle into "Literature."

So in a very short time everybody finally did know about Patrick O'Brian, to a degree that when he visited our shores he attracted a following of a dedication and willingness to travel great distances to be in The Presence that seems to me equaled only by that of the Grateful Dead or the Rolling Stones. And, like Mick Jagger, he never disappointed. What writer since Hemingway – and perhaps Fitzgerald – has looked so thoroughly the way you'd want him to? Clean-shaven, slim, slightly below middle height but giving the impression of that "wiry strength" more often found in novels than on the speaker's podium, and with the affect of bemusement that was, I think, a sort of courtesy to soften the impact of those daunting eyebrows and the comprehension, wit, and, occasionally, caustic scorn that flicked from him unceasingly. And then he was gone. Gone not merely from New York and Los Angeles and Seattle and all the other cities where people of high consequence were now wild to get him to their dinner parties, but from the world.

And yet, as the surprising volume you are holding reminds us, he is not gone at all. When death took Patrick O'Brian, this book had not been given a name. It had advanced only three chapters, 65 handwritten pages, most of which had been typed and given preliminary corrections by O'Brian (I say "preliminary" because there are, here and there, a few repetitions that this most scrupulous of writers would not have permitted himself). O'Brian in holograph offers advantages and drawbacks. I find his handwriting both exquisite and difficult to read, but persevering through it offers the pleasures of a wonderful bloodless duel that Stephen engineers, and a casual sketch of a seating arrangement that has the electrifying effect of making the principals seem entirely like living people. "21" is a fragment, of course, and one would expect such a document to be little more than a forlorn remnant. After all, O'Brian had been composing it during a melancholy time. His wife, Mary, had died; he was alone; he was eighty-five years old; and his newfound fame had brought his life under media scrutiny that would have dismayed people far less protective of their privacy than he.

But just look at "21"! There is no sense of harassment or desolation here, no loss of focus, nor of energy. And if it ends too soon, it is nonetheless a rich distillation – a summary of sorts – of all that has, over thousands of pages and tens of thousands of miles, won O'Brian such passionate admirers. First of all, there is the language – and here I mean not O'Brian's prose but what he gives his characters to say. He insisted that their speech was an accurate reflection of how early nineteenth-century people talked; but I believe it is a brilliant poetic invention, complex yet so wholly consistent that we in time learn to speak it almost through the same process we would follow acquiring a foreign language. It never ceases to show us that this is a world at once remote and familiar, and the conveying of that familiarity is, I think, a feat of the imagination that far surpasses, say, J.R.R. Tolkien's kingdoms of dwarfs and sorcerers.

We get to be introduced to Jack and Stephen one last time, and how keen the pleasure remains: Stephen abashed in the composition of his heavily-coded love letter; Jack with elephantine, ignorant delicacy discussing the Church of Rome with his closest friend. And here is Killick, his insolence for once extinguished by the calamity that has befallen Jack's best uniform during freezing weeks off the Horn. Now come the curiously stirring details: the men begging slush from the galley to give the shot in the garlands a pleasing sheen; Stephen clipping the tip of his pen "with a minute pair of metal jaws made for the purpose." To be sure, there's no battle in these pages, but the great-gun exercise on the Sussex gives a highly satisfactory sense of the violence and power that men like Jack Aubrey controlled. And any disappointment at the lack of a frigate duel must be eradicated by the presence of the humor that quietly leavens every paragraph. Jack, explaining how he acquired the extra gunpowder necessary for his spectacular exercise, says he'd bribed "the last powder-hoy, for a trifle of whiskey – you know the Irish drink, Stephen, I am sure?" "I have never heard of it," says Stephen. This tiny exchange is marvelously appealing: both men are being funny; both men understand one another perfectly.

Their amity suggests what I find so moving about this last work from Patrick O'Brian's hand. Some of the novels end with their principals settled and content, some with them in poverty and peril. It is, of course, impossible to say where "21" would have left them. I'm sure the egregious Captain Miller would have reappeared to work some malice after Stephen's humiliation of him. And Jack's money-making initiatives would likely have put him on the metaphorical lee-shore.

Right now, however, we are able to visit these friends we have followed so very far in a rare state of almost perfect felicity. Jack has seen his black son ably discharging important duties. Sophie and his daughters are with him; Brigid is with her father, she's thriving, and Stephen is with a woman who is very dear to him. Jack is flying a rear-admiral's flag aboard a ship of the line. So we can leave them sailing through fair, sweet days – Stephen with his dissections, Jack with his "sacred blue flag," Killick muttering darkly over the toasted cheese – embarked on a voyage like the one that opens the book: "Quietly indeed they sailed along, with gentle breezes that wafted them generally northwards at something in the nature of five miles in the hour, northwards to even warmer seas. Little activity was called for, apart from the nice adjustment of the sails, and although the exact routine of the ship was never relaxed nor her very strict rules of cleanliness, these long sunny days with a soldier's wind seemed to many the ideal of a seaman's life – regular, steady, traditional meals with the exact allowance of grog; hornpipes in the last dog-watch, the deep melody of the Doctor's 'cello from the cabin and the cheerful sound of the gunroom's dinner; the future lost in a haze somewhere north of the equator."

Remember that this was written at a time when the author was lonely and tormented. Yet Patrick O'Brian has given a farewell to his followers that is as gracious as it is gallant. And we, in turn, may find some solace in the thought that of all people, this man would not have hated to be taken out of action much as Nelson was: deep in triumph, shedding glory on the service he loved, and still at the peak of his powers.

Master and Commander

Master and Commander is the first of Patrick O'Brian's now famous Aubrey/Maturin novels, regarded by many as the greatest series of historical novels ever written. It establishes the friendship between Captain Jack Aubrey R. N. and Stephen Maturin, who becomes his secretive ship's surgeon and an intelligence agent. It contains all the action and excitement which could possibly be hoped for in a historical novel, but it also displays the qualities which have put O'Brian far ahead of any of his competitors: his depiction of the detail of life aboard a Nelsonic man-of-war, of weapons, food, conversation and ambience, of the landscape and of the sea. O'Brian's portrayal of each of these is faultless and the sense of period throughout is acute. His power of characterisation is above all masterly. This brilliant historical novel marked the debut of a writer who has grown into one of the most remarkable literary novelists now writing, the author of what Alan Judd, writing in the *Sunday Times*, has described as 'the most significant extended story since Anthony Powell's *A Dance to the Music of Time*'.

'It is as though, under Mr O'Brian's touch, those great sea-paintings at Greenwich had stirred and come alive.'

TOM POCOCK, *Evening Standard*

'*Master and Commander* recreates with delightful subtlety the flavour of life aboard a midget British man-of-war, plying the western Mediterranean in the year 1800, a year of indecisive naval skirmishes with France and Spain. Even for a reader not especially interested in matters nautical, the author's easy command of the philosophical, political, sensual and social temper of the times flavours a rich entertainment.'

MARTIN LEVIN, *New York Times Book Review*

ISBN: 978 0 00 649915 2

Post Captain

Post Captain is the second novel in Patrick O'Brian's remarkable Aubrey/Maturin series and led Mary Renault to write: *'Master and Commander* raised dangerously high expectations; *Post Captain* triumphantly surpasses them.'

The tale begins with Jack Aubrey arriving home from his exploits in the Mediterranean to find England at peace following the Treaty of Amiens. He and his friend Stephen Maturin, surgeon and secret agent, begin to live the lives of country gentlemen, punting, entertaining and enjoying more amorous adventures. Their comfortable existence, however, is cut short when Jack is overnight reduced to a pauper with enough debts to keep him in prison for life. He flees to the continent to seek refuge: instead he finds himself a hunted fugitive as Napoleon has ordered the internment of all Englishmen in France. Aubrey's adventures in escaping from France and the debtors' prison will grip the reader as fast as his unequalled actions at sea.

'Mr O'Brian is a master of his period, in which his characters are firmly placed, while remaining three-dimensional, intensely human beings. This book sets him at the very top of his genre … It is brilliant.'   MARY RENAULT

ISBN: 978 0 00 649916 9

H.M.S. Surprise

H.M.S. Surprise follows the variable fortunes of Captain Jack Aubrey's career in Nelson's navy as he attempts to hold his ground against admirals, colleagues and the enemy, accepting a commission to convey a British ambassador to the East Indies. The voyage takes him and his friend Stephen Maturin to the strange sights and smells of the Indian sub-continent, and through the archipelago of spice islands where the French have a near-overwhelming local superiority.

Rarely has a novel managed to convey more vividly the fragility of a sailing ship in a wild sea. Rarely has a historical novelist combined action and lyricism of style in the way that O'Brian does. His superb sense of place, brilliant characterisation and a vigour and joy of writing lifts O'Brian above any but the most exalted of comparisons.

'He is perhaps unique … in that his books can absorb and enthral landlubbers who do not even know the difference between 'a jib-boom and a taffrail.'

VALERIE WEBSTER, *Scotsman*

'*H.M.S. Surprise* is the third in the series, and one can hardly give it higher praise than to say that it maintains the level of the other two. The language is just right, with a full late eighteenth-century weightiness that is still free from any trace of strain or affectation.'   JULIAN SYMONS, *Sunday Times*

ISBN: 978 0 00 649917 6

The Mauritius Command

Captain Jack Aubrey is ashore, married with twin daughters, living in a damp cottage in Hampshire on half-pay and without a command – until Stephen Maturin arrives with secret orders for Aubrey to take the frigate, *Boadicea* to the Cape of Good Hope, under a Commodore's pennant. But the difficulties of carrying out his orders are compounded by two of his own captains – Lord Clonfert, a pleasure seeking dilettante, and Captain Corbett, whose severity can push his crews to the verge of mutiny.

'Patrick O'Brian has written splendid novels – of which *The Mauritius Command* is the latest – recounting episodes in the lives of the naval officer Jack Aubrey and his friend the saturnine Irish physician, Stephen Maturin ... Taken together, the novels are a brilliant achievement. They display staggering erudition on almost all aspects of early nineteenth-century life, with impeccable period detail.'

T.J. BINYON, *Times Literary Supplement*

'During the Napoleonic Wars, Captain Jack Aubrey reaches middle-age and is beached with domesticity: wife, daughters, mother-in-law, several servants, all packed into a little cottage like the Black Hole ... He jumps at the chance to escape. What's more, he'll be with some great old friends, including ship's surgeon Stephen Maturin – with whom he loves to fiddle two-part Mozart inventions over port in the ship's cabin.'   *Kirkus*

ISBN: 978 0 00 649918 3

Desolation Island

In *Desolation Island*, Jack Aubrey exchanges the Indian Ocean of *The Mauritius Command* for colder and lonelier seas. Commissioned to rescue Governor Bligh of Bounty fame, Jack Aubrey and Stephen Maturin sail the *Leopard* to Australia with a hold full of convicts. Among them is a beautiful and dangerous spy – and a treacherous disease which decimates the crew. The ingredients of a powerful and dramatic novel are heightened by descriptive writing of rare quality. Nowhere in contemporary prose has the majesty and terror of the sea been more effectively rendered than in the thrilling chase through an Antarctic storm in which Jack's ship, outmanned and outgunned, is the quarry not the hunter.

'Without intending sacrilege to C.S. Forester, for me Mr O'Brian's timbers are as sound, his historical soundings as deep, his power to impress and excite with the mystique of a ship under sail as great, and he packs more humour and writing into his books.' STEPHEN VAUGHAN, *Observer*

'Patrick O'Brian is a literary conjuror who can cure boredom with the flick of a pen. There is enough here to cure anything. When you start reading Jack Aubrey's adventures you will soon get to know that you are in for many a thrill and the occasional narrow squeak.' *Nautical Magazine*

'Seldom has it been my pleasure and thrill to have the terror and majesty of the sea more graphically depicted.'
Irish Independent

ISBN: 978 0 00 649924 4

The Fortune of War

As *The Fortune of War* opens Captain Jack Aubrey, R.N., sails the storm-beaten H.M.S. *Leopard* into harbour in the Dutch East Indies to find himself appointed to the command of the fastest and best-armed frigate in the Navy. He and Stephen Maturin take passage for England in a despatch vessel. But the War of 1812 against the United States breaks out while they are en route. Bloody actions precipitate them both into new and unexpected scenes where Stephen's past activities as a secret agent return on him with a vengeance.

'Captain Aubrey and his surgeon, Stephen Maturin, compose one of those complex and fascinating pairs of characters which have inspired thrilling stories of all kinds since the Iliad.'

JOHN BAYLEY, IRIS MURDOCH

ISBN: 978 0 00 649919 0

The Surgeon's Mate

Jack Aubrey and Stephen Maturin are ordered home by
despatch vessel to bring the news of their latest victory to the
government. But Maturin is a marked man for the havoc he has
wrought in the French intelligence network in the New World
and the attentions of two privateers soon become menacing.
The chase that follows through the fogs and shallows of the
Grand Banks is as thrilling, as tense and as unexpected in its cul-
mination as anything Patrick O'Brian has written. Then,
among other things, follows a shipwreck and a particularly sin-
ister internment in the notorious Temple Prison in Paris. Once
again the tigerish and fascinating Diana Villiers redresses the
balance in this man's world of seamanship and war.

'Captain Jack Aubrey and Stephen Maturin ... undertake a
secret mission in the Baltic; are later wrecked on the coast of
Brittany; are imprisoned in Paris, but are surreptitiously aided
to escape ... One must admire once again Patrick O'Brian's
subtle and persuasive re-creation of the past. Here there is
nothing of your ordinary historical novel ... instead each incident or description is saturated by a mass of complex and con-
vincing detail. Such details might be overwhelming ... were
they not reduced to their proper status as background by the
superabundant liveliness and lifelikeness of the characters;
and by the pace and excitement of the narrative. So eventful,
indeed, are the novels, it is easy to ignore the fact that ... they
are, on one level, addressing themselves to questions of
human actions and behaviour far beyond the compass of the
normal adventure story.'

T.J. BINYON, *Times Literary Supplement*

ISBN: 978 0 00 649921 3

The Ionian Mission

Jack Aubrey and Stephen Maturin, veterans of many battles, return in this novel to the seas where they first sailed as ship-mates. But Jack is now a senior Captain commanding a line-of-battle ship sent out to reinforce the squadron blockading Toulon, and this is a longer, harder, colder war than the dashing frigate actions of his early days. A sudden turn of events takes him and Stephen off on a hazardous mission to the Greek islands. All his old skills of seamanship and his prover-bial luck when fighting against odds come triumphantly into their own. The book ends with as fierce and thrilling an action as any in this magnificent series of novels.

'For Patrick O'Brian's followers, the arrival of a new Jack Aubrey–Stephen Maturin novel ranks with the events of a year. I know of no novelist who excites such fierce loyalty from a following which is almost a brotherhood in the intensity of its feelings for the writer and his works ... He is able to convey the detail of shipboard life without ever becoming tedious. Even when there is little action, when the plot is measured and easy, when he is merely describing a situation ... he never fails to keep the reader. His mastery is not limited to being a good writer. He is much more than that.'

KEVIN MYERS, *Irish Times*

ISBN: 978 0 00 649922 0

Treason's Harbour

Uniquely among authors of naval fiction, Patrick O'Brian allows his characters to develop with experience. The Jack Aubrey of *Treason's Harbour* has a record of successes equal to that of the most brilliant of Nelson's band of brothers, and he is no less formidable or decisive in action or strategy. But he is wiser, kinder, gentler too.

Much of the plot of *Treason's Harbour* depends on intelligence and counter-intelligence, a field in which Aubrey's friend Stephen Maturin excels. Through him we get a clearer insight into the life and habits of the sea officers of Nelson's time than we would ever obtain seeing things through their own eyes. There is plenty of action and excitement in this novel but it is the atmosphere of a Malta crowded with senior officers, waiting for news of what the French are up to and wondering whether the war will end before their turn comes for prize money and for fame, that is here so freshly and vividly conveyed.

'Patrick O'Brian's engaging Captain Jack Aubrey is the best thing afloat since Horatio Hornblower and notably less austere ashore.'
STEPHEN VAUGHAN, *Observer*

ISBN: 978 0 00 649923 7

The Far Side of the World

It is still the War of 1812. Patrick O'Brian takes his hero Jack
Aubrey and his tetchy, sardonic friend Stephen Maturin on a
voyage as fascinating as anything he has ever written. They set
course across the South Atlantic to intercept a powerful
American frigate outward bound to play havoc with the British
whaling trade. If they do not come up with her before she
rounds the Horn they must follow her into the Great South
Sea and as far across the Pacific as she may lead them. It is a
commission after Jack's own heart. Maturin has fish of his own
to fry in the world of secret intelligence.

Aubrey has to cope with a succession of disasters – men overboard, castaways, encounters with savages, storms, typhoons,
groundings, shipwrecks, to say nothing of murder and criminal
insanity. That the enemy is in fact faithfully dealt with no-one
who has the honour of Captain Aubrey's acquaintance can
take leave to doubt.

'All true lovers of the sea will find this a most enjoyable book.'
Nautical Magazine

'Aubrey has rarely undertaken a more hazardous mission or
one more packed with exciting incident.'   *Gloucester Citizen*

ISBN: 978 0 00 649925 1

The Reverse of the Medal

The Reverse of the Medal is in all respects an unconventional naval tale. Jack Aubrey returns from his duties protecting whalers off South America and is persuaded by a casual acquaintance to make investments in the City on the strength of supposedly certain information. From there he is led into the half-worlds of the London criminal underground and of government espionage – the province of his friend, Stephen Maturin, on whom alone he can rely.

Those who are already devoted readers of Patrick O'Brian will find here all the brilliance of characterisation and sparkle of dialogue which they have come to expect. For those who will read him for the first time there will be the pleasure of discovering, quite unexpectedly, a novelist of unique character.

'Taken together the novels are a brilliant achievement. They display staggering erudition on almost all aspects of eighteenth century life, with impeccable period detail.'

Times Literary Supplement

'These books are works of scholarship, classics of contemporary literature, joys to read. Savour *The Reverse of the Medal* and seek out its predecessors. You rob yourself by neglecting them.'

Western Morning News

ISBN: 978 0 00 649926 8

The Letter of Marque

Jack Aubrey is a naval officer, a post-captain of experience and capacity. When *The Letter of Marque* opens he has been struck off the Navy List for a crime he has not committed, and, because he is the man he is, there is no position that could cause him greater unhappiness. With Aubrey is his friend and ship's surgeon Stephen Maturin, who is also an unofficial British intelligence agent. Maturin has bought for Aubrey his old ship the *Surprise* so that the misery of ejection from the service can be palliated by the command of what Aubrey calls 'a private man-of-war' – a letter of marque, a privateer. Together they sail on a voyage which, if successful might restore Aubrey to the rank, and the raison d'etre whose loss he so much regrets.

Around these simple, ostensibly familiar elements Patrick O'Brian has written a novel of great narrative power, exploring his extraordinary world once more, in a tale full of human feeling and rarely matched in its drama.

'Delicacy and generosity of feeling are constant themes in O'Brian's novels. *The Letter of Marque* is both serious and light-hearted, true and sentimental, as comic opera can be.'
London Review ofBooks

'He does not just have the chief qualifications of a first-class historical novelist, he has them all.' MARY REANAULT

ISBN: 978 0 00 649927 5

The Thirteen-Gun Salute

As *The Thirteen-Gun Salute* opens Jack Aubrey has been rein-
stated to his command, and he and his old friend Dr Maturin
are sailing on a secret mission with a hand-picked crew, most
of them ship-mates from the adventures and lucrative voyages
of earlier years. But Patrick O'Brian's resourcefulness is a sure
warrant that things will not turn out as his readers or his characters expect. Twists and turns, sub-plots, echoes from the
past, these are the only certainties in this astonishing *roman
fleuve*. Distant waters, exotic scenes, flora and fauna to satisfy
Maturin's innocent curiosity as well as scope for his cloak and
dagger work enrich its flow. The ending of the book leaves the
reader more than usually impatient for its successor.

'In *The Thirteen-Gun Salute* we sail on a secret mission to the
East with those two devoted and disparate shipmates Aubrey
and Maturin, characters not tacked on to their period but
inhabiting it as completely as though the author were their
contemporary. For those unlucky enough not to have crossed
their bows, Captain Aubrey is a lion afloat and a bit of a lost
sheep ashore, Stephen Maturin, surgeon, naturalist, secret
agent … is an innocent of a different stamp; their friendship,
developed with subtlety and feeling, is an endearing and
enduring achievement. Here Aubrey is restored to the Navy
List, French intrigues in Malaysia are attacked, and Maturin
has a wonderful time, conveyed with a real sense of wonder,
among the strange flora and fauna.'

CHRISTOPHER WORDSWORTH, *Guardian*

ISBN: 978 0 00 649928 2

The Nutmeg of Consolation

Patrick O'Brian is regarded by many as the greatest living historical novelist writing in English. In *The Nutmeg of Consolation*, Jack Aubrey and Stephen Maturin begin stranded on an uninhabited island in the Dutch East Indies, attacked by ferocious Malay pirates. They contrive their escape, but after a stay in Batavia and a change of ship they are caught up in a night chase in fiercely tidal waters and then embroiled in the much more insidious conflicts of the terrifying penal settlements of New South Wales. It is one of O'Brian's most accomplished and gripping books.

'*The Nutmeg of Consolation* brings his achievement to a new height. Any contemporary novelist should recognize in Patrick O'Brian a Master of the Art.'   ALAN JUDD, *Sunday Telegraph*

'In length the series is unique; as far as quality is concerned, it cannot but be ranked with the best of twentieth-century historical novels.'   T.J. BINYON, *Independent*

ISBN: 978 0 00 649929 9

Clarissa Oakes

As *Clarissa Oakes* opens, Captain Jack Aubrey, a lion in action but somewhat at sea on land, sails away from the hated Australian prison colonies in his favourite vessel the *Surprise*, pondering as he does so on middle age and sexual frustration. He soon becomes aware that he is out of touch with the mood of his ship: to his astonishment he finds that in spite of a lifetime's experience he does not know what the foremost hands or even his own officers are thinking. They know, as he does not, that the *Surprise* has a stranger aboard: and what they, for their part, do not know is that the stranger is potentially as dangerous as a light in the powder magazine itself.

The author is a master of tension. A chase by an ostensibly friendly but strangely persistent cutter, the swell of disorder in the ship's company and the unpredictability of her captain's reactions carry the reader forward to a fierce battle on a Pacific island full of the drama and colour which his admirers have come to expect.

'Few books so entertaining and readable are based on such strong research and grasp of human nature. One moment you laugh aloud at comedy rooted in character, and the next, storming adventure or danger grips you by the throat ... good writing allied to must-read-on storytelling.'

SHAUN USHER, *Daily Mail*

'What is so gripping about O'Brian's novels is the completeness with which he invents a world which is our own and not our own ... O'Brian is a brilliant observer.'

A. S. BYATT, *Evening Standard*

ISBN: 978 0 00 649930 5

The Wine-Dark Sea

At the opening of a voyage filled with disaster and delight, Jack Aubrey and Stephen Maturin are in pursuit of a privateer sailing under American colours through the Great South Sea. Stephen's objective is to set the revolutionary tinder of South America ablaze to relieve the pressure on the British government which, already engaged in a death-struggle with a Europe dominated by Napoleon, has blundered into war with the young and uncomfortably vigorous United States.

The shock and barbarity of hand-to-hand fighting are sharpened by O'Brian's exact sense of period, his eye for landscape and his feel for a ship under sail. His thrilling descriptions of hair-raising and bloody actions make the reader grateful that he is watching from a distance.

'To read Patrick O'Brian is to turn the pages of literary history. His series of novels comprises the most significant extended story since Anthony Powell's *A Dance to the Music of Time*.'

ALAN JUDD, *Sunday Times*

'O'Brian has shown us that in our literary silver age, authentic gold can still be mined … He is a man whose books you would dare to give Sterne; whose conversation would have delighted Coleridge. It is his misfortune, but our great good luck, that he is our contemporary, and not theirs.'

WILLIAM WALDEGRAVE, *The Times*

ISBN: 978 0 00 649931 2

The Commodore

Jack Aubrey's long service is at last rewarded: he is promoted to the rank of Commodore, and given a squadron of ships to command. His mission is twofold – to make a large dent in the slave trade off the coast of Africa and, on his return, to intercept a French fleet set for Bantry Bay with a cargo of weapons for the disaffected among the Irish.

But might the nature of the secret mission on which the squadron is sent present a conflict of loyalties for the complicated and inscrutable figure of Stephen Maturin, Jack's indispensable ship's surgeon and close friend? Invention and surprise follow at every turn in this tale of nineteenth-century seamanship, as rich, as compelling, as masterly as any of its predecessors.

'While his stories tell of men at war, he is a novelist of great gentleness of spirit. A pervasive serenity, a generosity towards human frailty, are among the qualities which have made his books irresistible … All the familiar virtues of O'Brian are here: effortless command of period dialogue, seamanship, culture and manners: intimate understanding of a small floating world dominated by the vagaries of the wind; droll observation of human idiosyncrasy …'   MAX HASTINGS, *Daily Telegraph*

'In English fiction my chief pleasures this year came from reading four books in the series about Captain Jack Aubrey, RN by Patrick O'Brian, a writer whose work I have discovered late in the day, and who writes the sort of elegant, civilized and humorous prose that ought, in my opinion, just now and then to win the Booker Prize.'

                    JAN MORRIS, *Independent Books of the Year*

ISBN: 978 0 00 649932 9